ß A

Tempting

~~ Campus Heat Series ~~

M.D. Dalrymple

Tempting

Copyright 2021 M.D. Dalrymple
ISBN: 9798715970374
Imprint: Independently published

Cover art and formatting by M.D. Dalrymple

Tempting

If you love this book, be sure to leave a review! Reviews are life blood for authors, and I appreciate every review I receive!

Love what you read? Want more from Michelle? Click the image below to receive Gavin, the free Glen Highland Romance short ebook, plus two more free ebooks, updates, and more in your inbox

https://linktr.ee/mddalrympleauthor

Tempting

Table of Contents

Tempting

Chapter One

SABRINA WALKED INTO the writing center in a flustered huff. Today had started so well, especially after the past few weeks.

Her old-fashioned, "You aren't one of those empowered females" type boyfriend was finally done. She had almost slapped him when he said he believed women were supposed to be submissive.

What the hell? Was he stuck in the 1950s? She wasn't looking for a Mrs. Degree at MLC!

Evan just didn't get it. And he wasn't worth the air it took to explain it to him.

Tempting

Who today thinks he can get away with that? Not with Sabrina Alonto. That's for certain.

They had broken up a while ago, and he'd tried a few times to hook up with her and had finally gotten the hint after she blocked his number. Now he was done, gone, and for the past several weeks, life had improved significantly. Even today, a bright and sunny Southern California day, mirrored her exuberance as she got out of bed.

She had been feeling good, dammit! She was getting As in her classes, including Professor Antez's stats class. The semester was almost over – finals were next week, so all she had to do was hang on until then. And to make sure she could still work at the writing center over summer, she enrolled in the impacted Soc 200 course and got in! Everything was going so well.

Then, just as things were looking up, they slammed back down. It was like the universe saved up all its karma and unloaded it on her before noon.

First, her roommate Diana said she couldn't afford to stay in the apartment over the summer. *What the hell?* How was Sabrina supposed to pay for the rent alone? And there was no way she'd find a roommate who needed a three-month lease over the summer.

Fuckery number 1.

Then her computer ate her English paper. She was almost done, and she had her previous saved version, but all her revisions were gone. *Gone*! It was due tomorrow, so now she'd have to pull an all-nighter after her shift at the writing center to get it done.

Fuckery number 2.

And she almost didn't make it to campus anyway – her car stalled twice before turning over, and Sabrina had no idea what was going on. The car wasn't even that old, and she'd taken it in for an oil change last month. Once she was parked on campus, she dialed the local repair shop, and they said they could get her in tomorrow.

And there was Fuckery number 3.

Sabrina's mind was on her car and how she hoped it started when it was time to leave the writing center, and she didn't notice her two o'clock appointment waiting by the small conference room door in the library.

"Tannis! I'm sorry. Am I late?"

Sabrina juggled her backpack and her purse, trying to check the time. Clocking in late would be the cherry on top of this miserable day.

"No, no. Class got out early, so you're all good. Don't apologize."

He gave her one of his winning smiles, a smile straight from a toothpaste commercial. That, with his cinnamon-blond hair, sky-blue eyes, and his athletic physique, it was no wonder he was one of the most sought-after guys on campus. Either as a friend or to date.

And it fed the rumors that he was a thirst trap and a player.

The thirst trap she could understand. Too often she found herself daydreaming about him after their tutoring sessions, wondering if that amber sprinkle of freckles appeared elsewhere on his body.

But as a player? Sabrina didn't have time for that. Plus, she wasn't the popular, go-to-all-the-games-and-parties type, so she wasn't *his* type.

Popular baseball players didn't go for the smart girls.

She still admired his handsome body and the relaxed way he held himself. Christ, he didn't have a care in the world.

Must be nice.

Sabrina took a deep breath and flashed a tight smile to Tannis.

"Ok, then why don't you grab a seat and get your paper, and I'll join you as soon as I clock in."

With that smile, Tannis could melt butter. A panty dropper for certain.

"Sure thing, boss!"

Oh, to have such a nonchalant attitude, not a worry in the world like that lovely man.

After the morning she'd had, Sabrina wasn't sure she could handle his positivity. It was almost too much. She sighed. It wouldn't be the first time she wore a fake smile for the day.

"Ok, so here is what you need to fix. Remember when Professor L said you need to have more than one sentence for your intro and your conclusion?"

Tannis studied the paper on the table and bit his lip. No, he didn't remember. Was his thesis sentence in the introduction? What else did it need?

"I guess I don't remember that. What do I need to put in the intro? Or the conclusion?"

Sabrina tried not to let her aggravation show on her face as she grabbed her info sheet from her backpack. How did teachers deal with students like this? She had a newfound respect for her professors and vowed she would never become one.

Tannis's eyes remained on his paper. Writing had never been his strong suit. So many rules, so many ways to get it right or do it wrong. Sabrina placed a colorful sheet on the table.

"See here?" She pointed with a chipped nail polished finger. "This shows some of the things you can add to craft your introduction. Do any of these look like they might work?"

Tannis reviewed the sheet, picked ideas to add to his introduction and conclusion, and made notes on his paper. Sabrina remembered all these little rules, wrote papers that met the page requirements, and made it look so simple.

"Ok, Tannis, we're just about done. Any more questions?"

Look at her, sitting across from me with an air of confidence. I bet she doesn't have to worry about failing any of her classes and losing her scholarship. Tannis bit his lip, afraid of her answer to his question.

"Do you think it's good enough to get a C? Or even a B? Lenski can be a tough grader."

"Yeah, but only on certain things. As long as you are nailing those, you can do pretty well in her class."

Tannis's chest burned. "Did I nail any of those things?" He hated the hesitance in his voice, and Professor L was a great teacher, but his anxiety was real. Tannis needed to pass this class.

"Fixing the intro and conclusion will help. Are you worried about your grade? You've met with me for two other essays, and you said you did Ok on those. I would think that means you can get a C in the class, easy."

Slouching in his metal chair, Tannis huffed out a sarcastic laugh. "Yeah, you'd think so. But I've missed some homework, and I tanked that first paper. It's why she recommended I come here."

Sabrina's wise, sable eyes scrutinized him like he was under a microscope as she leaned forward on the table. "You can always take the class again, if you fail."

Tannis shook his head. "Doesn't work that way. I have a baseball scholarship. Not a huge one, but it makes up the difference for what I can't pay for college. If I lose that, I'm not playing ball anymore, mostly because I won't be here."

She leaned forward even more, her attentive eyes mesmerizing him. Sabrina had a way of looking at someone as though they were the only person in the room. And right now, that intense gaze was on him. His bravado slipped under that gaze.

"What are you saying? That if you don't do well on this paper, you might not pass Professor L's class? You might lose your scholarship?"

For the first time since Sabrina started tutoring Tannis, his bravado faltered, and he dipped his head so she wouldn't see the abashed look on his face.

Life had always come easy to Tannis – friends, sports, even school, if he got the right teachers in easier classes. He kept his nose clean and made what his parents considered "smart choices." And it formed the foundation of his identity, his swagger, what he expected of himself.

But three classes, most specifically this English class . . . He was on the losing side of the college battle. And if he didn't play ball next year and couldn't go to college, then who was he, in truth?

His buddy Damon worked on cars, and if Damon needed a job, he could find one easily in any repair shop. Tannis didn't have anything like that. All he was great at was playing ball.

He needed it. There was nothing for him if not baseball.

"Yeah," he answered with a deep breath. "Yeah. I am. Professor L is a decent prof. And she's dating Coach, so I might get some pity points, but this final paper. I won't lie, Sabrina, I am really, like *really*, worried."

She gave him a squinty-eyed gaze, measuring him up. *Does she think I'm lying? That I'm not being honest?*

If he weren't so anxious about this paper, he might have cared. As it was, he waited while she evaluated him. It had been a long time since anyone tried to measure him up as something other than a ball player.

"I can see it. And I don't blame you. College is expensive. It's why I'm here. And I have to keep my GPA up, too, to keep my academic scholarship."

Sabrina reached out and patted his arm as he sagged against the hard library chair.

"Well, I also need to ask if you are working over the summer?" he asked. "My parents want me to take a class over summer, to keep me on top of school, you know? I was

13

planning on taking my psych requirements, but I heard from some other guys on the team that most of the classes have at least one large paper, or more depending on the professor. Can you help me with that class?"

She straightened in her seat. "You're good with what we're doing? With how I'm helping you?"

His eyebrows scrunched together. "Well, yeah. I'm here now, aren't I? Twice a week near paper due dates?"

"That's true." Sabrina tapped her pen on his scuffed-up pages. "Yeah, I'm here over the summer. But let's work on this paper here and get you through Professor L's class. How does that sound?"

Her smile was full, reshaping her whole face into a beautifully relaxed version of Sabrina she had never exhibited in class. Full pink lips curving over a perfectly straight set of teeth that had to be the result of braces and curled into clear cheeks. A surprising warmth spread through Tannis at that rare smile, and he paused, wondering where that came from.

He'd thought her cute when he first met her in class. He'd nudged his desk-mate Cory and told him so. But that smile. Did she know how stunning it made her? How brilliant? Maybe it was because she displayed it so rarely. Maybe that was why she wore a serious expression all the time.

While he was distracted, her silky black hair swung into her face as she tapped his paper again.

"Tannis?"

"Yeah," he said in a clipped voice, regaining his focus. "Yeah, let's get this paper done. I'm putty in your masterful hands."

Tannis grinned his best, *why yes I am an adorable star baseball player* grin, hoping to encourage Sabrina to smile back.

Her smile was dangerous. He could easily lose track of his tutoring, distracting as she was.

But sitting there at the writing center table with her, it didn't matter.

Tannis vowed to do everything he could to have her smile at him again.

Tempting

Chapter Two

SIX O'CLOCK ARRIVED too fast, especially when Sabrina had a full roster of students to tutor. At least most of her students were at the English 100 level, so her brain went on autopilot for the afternoon.

She signed her timecard for the day and tucked it into its slot. *So low-tech,* she thought, which was odd since the computer lab was one doorway from the room where her timecard was located. Dr. Kane, who ran the writing lab, had promised they would be on a computer timecard system next semester.

I'll believe it when I see it, Sabrina thought.

Her mind was on the writing center and her own paper that she needed to finish before class in the morning when she got into her modest hatchback. The parking lot was still fairly bright, the sun arcing in its final descent in the horizon, and students milled about. That was a perk to her tutoring. Except for about two months in the winter, it was usually daylight when she walked out to her car after work.

She tossed her PINK backpack onto the passenger seat, stabbed her key into the ignition, and turned.

Clicking sounds, then nothing.

Her chest shuddered. *No, no, no, no . . .*

Making sure she was pressing the brake all the way to the floor, Sabrina inhaled hard through her nose and turned the key again.

Another series of clicking.

Fuck.

She dropped her forehead to her steering wheel. At least she knew her car trouble was her battery. How much did a new one cost? Hopefully it wasn't too expensive.

How am I supposed to get home? How am I going to get this car to the shop for a new battery?

A tow truck was out of the question. She didn't have the money for a battery – how in the hell would she pay for a tow?

FUCK.

A tapping at her window yanked her from her frustrated concentration, and she sat up in a flash of panic.

Tannis was bent over at her window, his easy smile directed at her. She had to open the car door because the window wouldn't roll down. Tannis filled out his baseball shirt, which was filthy with dirt, and had a blue duffel in his hand. His baseball cap covered most of his tawny hair. He must have just finished at practice.

"Hey. I saw you sitting here. Car trouble?"

Sabrina opened her mouth to say everything was fine and she'd handle it, but her mouth snapped shut so fast her teeth clacked. Everything was *not* fine, and she'd be a fool to think Tannis hadn't seen that.

"Yeah. I think it's my battery. It just makes a clicking sound when I put the key in."

Tannis's face brightened. What was he so happy about? She was stuck!

"How about a jump?"

Sabrina pulled her head back to stare up at him. "What?"

Tannis pointed to the front of her car. "A jump. You ever get a jump before? I got cables in my car. I'll park here next to you and we will get it going. Hold on."

Before she could respond, he was jogging off full of cocky confidence, and Sabrina didn't stop herself from staring at his tight backside as he ran to his car.

Stop, she told herself. *You don't need a player. He's only being nice because you're his tutor.*

Still, that view.

Tannis's blue sedan wasn't much nicer than hers, but it ran. He shut the car off, clicked his hood release, and came over to her with red and black cables in his hand.

"Pop your hood," he directed, and she yanked on the knob with the image of the open hood.

Tannis went right to work, and Sabrina felt like a stereotype as she stood next to him and watched him with his hands in her engine. She justified it as learning how to attach the cables, so next time she'd know what to do.

"Ok, I'll start my car then you start yours."

She sat in her car, and even though Tannis seemed to know what he was doing, a wave of doubt flared in Sabrina. *With the shit day this has been, it probably won't work –*

Her car roared to life at the turn of the key.

Sabrina smiled at Tannis as he ran to the front of their cars to pull off the cables.

"Thank you so much," she told him as she stood at her door. Tannis tossed the cables through the open window in his car.

"Of course. That'll keep you for a while, unless you need a new battery."

Sabrina clenched her lips together before speaking.

"Um, do you know how much a battery will cost?"

She hated asking, but she wanted to be prepared for the sticker shock.

Tannis's ocean blue eyes regarded her, then he smiled that lazy smile again. How did he smile so easily? Sabrina's eyes were hot with tears and here he wore this tempting smile!

"Tell you what. I can save you some money maybe. Do you know how to install a battery?"

"What? No! I didn't even know how to do the jump!"

"Ok. Give me a minute."

Tannis pulled his phone from the pocket of his jeans and punched at the screen. He held up one finger in a *wait a minute* gesture, and when the phone dinged, he tapped at the screen again.

"Here's the deal. Are you busy right now? I just texted my buddy, Damon. He works on cars. I'll follow you over to the car parts store, give you another jump if you need it, and then you can follow me to Damon's. He'll put that battery in for you in no time."

Sabrina chewed at her bottom lip as she considered Tannis's offer. It had to be cheaper than a repair shop.

"How much will it cost me? For your friend to do it for me?"

His swoon-worthy smile curled to the left. "Nothing. He'll put it in for free. You only have to get the battery."

"Are you sure? that seems like a lot to do for free."

Tannis flapped his hand at her to dismiss her protest.

"Naw. We do favors for each other all the time. He's cool. Let's do this."

The sun was entering the gray area above the horizon, and as much as she didn't have the time, what with her paper waiting for her at home, she also couldn't pass up free car labor. Sabrina nodded.

"That's a great idea. Thank you so much, Tannis. You didn't have to do this."

He pressed his hand to his chest and feigned a look of indignation.

"What kind of person do you think I am? To leave you stranded? Never! I'm enjoying this. Now I get to see who Sabrina is outside of class and tutoring."

She pursed her lips again, and a hot flush warmed her skin, but he didn't wait for her answer. He winked at her and jogged to his driver's side door.

Sabrina got into her car and slammed the door.

She's not much more exciting than what you get in class, she lamented and put the car in reverse.

Tannis followed Sabrina to Tiny's Auto Parts, which was fortunately a mile down the street. He had checked the date on her battery, and from the "ohhhh," breath he emitted, she assumed her battery was older than was safe. She was lucky it had lasted as long as it did.

He walked her inside, carried her new purchase to her car and put it on the floor of her passenger seat. With his engaging smile, he told her to follow him. Before he left the side of her car, he pulled out his phone.

"Why don't you give me your number? I'll text you the address just in case we get separated."

She rattled off her number, and her phone dinged right after with his text. Then he knocked on the hood of her car and climbed into his. His friend Damon was a few streets from the auto store.

Tannis parked in the street and waved her into the brightly lit driveway of the dumpy-looking house surrounded by a chain link fence in the student housing neighborhood. Then he hustled to the door and knocked. A shorter young man with slick black hair joined Tannis on the driveway. The garage door was already open.

"Sabrina, this is Damon."

She tipped her head and gave him a tight smile. Her stomach flipped at her using someone she didn't know for car service.

"Hey, Sabrina. My boy here says you need a new battery. Did you get one? Pop the hood. I'll grab my tools and get it in for you."

Sabrina mouthed *thanks* as he turned toward the garage. She popped her hood open while Tannis lifted the battery from her car.

She lingered at the side of her car and curiously watched as Damon ducked into her engine and swapped out the old battery for the new one in just a few minutes. Tannis served as Damon's assistant, handing him tools and exchanging the batteries. They were done just as it became full dark.

"See?" Tannis, with his eternal smile, slammed down the hood. "I told you my boy would take care of it and you only had to pay for the battery. Hey, Damon! How much would that have cost at a shop?"

Damon wiped his hands on a rag from his garage. "Depending on where you went, fifty to seventy-five bucks for the labor. Up-charge for the battery."

"Well, thanks, man. I owe you one."

"You always do, man." Damon smacked Tannis's arm.

"Yeah, thanks Damon," Sabrina added in a tentative voice.

He'd just saved her so much time and money, and he didn't even know her. Hell, Tannis barely knew her. She felt like she was in one of those old Twilight Zone shows her mom used to watch. Lucky things like this just didn't happen to Sabrina, but maybe she deserved it after the shit morning she had.

"You want to come in? Have a drink?" Damon cocked his dark head to the door.

She hated to be impolite, but her unsaved paper needed her attention, and it was getting late.

"I'd like to, but I — we — have this paper due tomorrow, and I had a computer glitch that didn't auto save like it was supposed to."

Damon shrugged. "Tannis?"

"Shit man, didn't you hear her say that we have a paper due tomorrow? Are you playing me like that in front of my tutor?"

Damon nodded and rubbed his fingers along his chin. "Nice. I didn't know tutors could look like that."

"Damon!"

Really, they were talking about her as if she weren't here? Fucking misogyny. Then Tannis turned to her. No smile, earnest eyes. Wow, she hadn't expected that.

"I'm sorry, Sabrina. You're sorry too, right, Damon?"

Damon had enough sense to look abashed as he nodded again.

"Yeah, I'm sorry. I didn't mean anything by it. I guess I just made an assumption."

His apology came as a surprise. Maybe he *was* redeemable.

"Not a big deal. Thanks for the apology, though."

"Hey, why don't you come by Saturday night. We're having a party."

Damon's invitation was yet another surprise. Sabrina wasn't exactly a party type girl.

"What? Really?"

A bright-toothed grin flashed across Damon's face. He jerked a thumb at Tannis. "Yeah! My boy Tannis will be there. You should come."

"Yeah, you should," Tannis agreed. "And if you want to bring friends or anything, you can. If it makes you feel safer or, uh, you know . . ."

"Like I'm at a party where I don't know anyone?"

Tannis pressed his palm against his jaw and a touch of pink colored his cheeks.

Is he blushing?

"Um, yeah. but you'll know me. And Damon."

"And Damon," she parroted, biting the inside of her cheek so as not to smile at his awkwardness.

"Yeah, and me," Damon's deep voice piped up. "It's my house."

Sabrina flicked her eyes toward the ramshackle house. It was the end of the semester. Her final papers would be done this week, and she had two other final exams next week. This week, so much stress. A party would be a great stress-reliever. *Why not?* Diana was always up for a good time and knew a lot of the same people Tannis did – she could probably come with her. Sabrina made a mental note of who else she might invite. Jana from stats, for certain. And Adele from her literature class might want to go as well.

"Sabrina?" Tannis's voice interrupted her thoughts.

"Yeah. Yes. I have a few friends who might want to join me. If you're Ok with that, we'll be here."

Damon's face lit up. "Great! Any time after seven. Park in the street."

He clapped Tannis on the back.

"See you Saturday, man."

"You too, Damon, and thanks again."

"Yes, thanks again!" Sabrina added, throwing her hand in the air in a graceless wave.

Damon went back to his garage, and Tannis opened her driver's side door.

"Ok, I know you have a paper to finish – "

"You, too. Good luck on it Tannis. I hope you do well." Sabrina folded herself into the driver's seat.

"Yeah. I need the luck. See you in class tomorrow morning."

He slammed the door, and she gave him a quick wave before backing out the drive and heading for her apartment.

Sabrina burst through the door to the well-lit living room where Diana was watching TV and eating left over pizza.

"Diana! Guess what just happened to me!" she squealed.

Chapter Three

"I'M GLAD YOU aren't mad at me about having to move back home for the summer," Diana told her. "And I'm glad to be going to this party with you."

Diana sat on the couch, finishing a plate that had salad leavings on it. Sabrina's roommate had been unbelievably contrite over the past week after letting Sabrina know about the change in plans. While she hadn't solved the summer roommate problem yet, Sabrina hoped the landlord might cut her a break since she was staying through the next year, and Diana was going to return in late August. She had also offered to help Sabrina with part of the rent, so there was that.

Plus, she and Diana had known each other since middle school. They weren't the best of friends in high school but grew close over the summer before college started. Rooming together seemed natural, and neither had any deal-breaking habits that made living together a problem.

Truthfully, much of Diana's appreciation for Sabrina stemmed from the fact that most of Sabrina's frustrations earlier in the week had been fixed. Her car, some of the roommate problem, and her paper just flowed when she finished it, and she got to bed at a decent hour.

Sabrina was actually in a terrific mood. Better than she'd felt most of the semester.

"I get it, Diana. It sucks, but at least it's only a couple of months."

"Oh, here." Diana unfolded her shockingly long legs from under herself on the couch and grabbed her purse off the counter. "I just got paid, and I promised I'd help as much as I could. It's a hundred. You deserve so much more for this shit position I put you in."

While a hundred wasn't the four hundred she needed to make up Diana's share of the rent, the landlord would probably take it if it meant keeping a pair of neat, quiet renters.

"Thanks, Diana. This will help a lot."

Diana's lips thinned almost to non-existent, and her deep blue eyes lit up. She had always been the more emotional, more sensitive of the two of them. Get her angry however . . .

"I'm going to finish putting on my makeup and getting dressed for this shin-ding, now that you're home. I nuked some chicken nuggets. And I made sure there's some salad in the fridge for you."

Diana's long form sauntered to her bedroom door, and not for the first time, a flash of fiery green jealousy sparked in Sabrina. Long legs, long body – the MLC volleyball team was fortunate in Diana. And she'd made dinner?

"You're gonna make a basketball player a great wife one day, Di!"

Diana's hand flapped from her doorway as her giggle carried to the kitchen where Sabrina made a small plate for dinner.

Right after eight, they drove the short distance to student housing. Diana's interest in Sabrina's connection to this party meant she didn't shut up with the questions for the entire ride.

"So, this Damon guy, just invited you? And you don't know him?"

Sabrina brushed her black fringe of hair from the side of her head as she glanced over her shoulder to make the turn.

"Well, Tannis invited me, too."

"Yeah. *Tannis.*" Diana flashed a knowing smile at Sabrina.

"It's not like that. I'm his tutor. He helped me out with my car. That's it."

Diana dropped her head to the head rest.

"You are much stronger and more outgoing and attractive than you give yourself credit for. And I don't believe your denial for a minute. He's a hottie."

"He's a player."

"No, he's not," Diana flipped the visor down to check her make-up. Sabrina pulled along the curb. "Ugh, student housing is like a ghetto."

29

"A drunk, party ghetto," Sabrina agreed as she shut off the car. "And what do you mean he's not a player? He's a baseballer, and he flirts with everyone, goes to every party. I've heard he dates any girl he sees. What do you mean he's not a player?"

"Sabrina, you got to let go of the stereotypes." Diana flipped the visor back up and tipped her head toward the house. "Why don't you find out?"

The din of pounding music trailed down the street to where Sabrina had parked. Diana's words spun in her head. Tannis was an athlete, the big campus jock – weren't all those guys players?

Sabrina shouldn't have been surprised when they walked through the warped gray door to find the party full of student athletes. Her heart sunk in her chest – other than Tannis and Diana, she wouldn't know anyone here.

Worse, she felt like she was a munchkin in the Emerald City. All these tall, fit people who were tight friends. Even though she thought she looked cute in her cropped white shirt and plaid skirt, seeing everyone in their tight jeans and tanks made her question her choice. Sabrina was the short, awkward cousin to Diana's presence.

"Di! Hey! I didn't know you were coming!" A tall, darker-skinned young woman with a head full of perfectly aligned braids ran up to Diana and hugged her. Another volleyball player.

Yep, I don't fit in.

Sabrina wished that Jada or Adele had been able to come, but they both had other plans. Adele had texted her a

30

quick *good luck* before Sabrina had left the apartment. Diana grabbed her arm.

"Come on, Brin! Let's get a drink and start dancing!"

Sabrina put on a huge, fake smile. "You go. I'm going to see if I can find Tannis."

"Tannis?" The volleyball girl asked. "He's over there." Her long, shockingly toned arm pointed toward the far side of the room.

"Thanks," Sabrina said as Diana and the woman laughed their way toward the kitchen.

The pounding music thundered in her ears, shaking her brain, as she weaved through the dim light and thick crowd, looking for the well-built, tawny haired Tannis. She found him standing by the sliding glass back door, talking to Damon, a red cup in hand. His eyes caught on her as she walked up and widened with his smile.

"Hey! Sabrina! You made it!" He leaned in and gave her a quick peck on the cheek. If it hadn't already been so hot, they would have seen her blush.

"Yeah," she breathed, pushing wisps of her black hair from her damp face. A slight breeze blew in from the open door, and she was grateful for the cooling breath it provided.

"Hey, Sabrina," Damon said, holding up a fist.

Sabrina gave it a bump and a genuine smile finally appeared on her face. Damon seemed like a fist-bump guy, and she clung to that measure of certainty to relax her nerves. Everything else about this party screamed uncertainty. At least for her.

"Let me introduce you to some other people. You might know them. A few are in our English class with us."

He enveloped her hand in his large, warm one, and a lightness bubbled up in Sabrina's chest. *He's holding my hand? At a party? What the hell?*

Most likely just another notch on his belt, but she didn't question it further. Instead, she tried to release some of her inhibitions and let Tannis take the lead.

They made their way to the back yard, where a few tables and decaying patio chairs sat atop the cracked patio. A group of guys sat in several of the chairs by the firepit, talking and laughing.

"Hey, Reyes!" one of the guys hollered as they approached.

"Hey, Gabe. This is Sabrina, my tutor I told you about. Sabrina, this is Gabe, Alonso, Enrique, and Romeo." Each one lifted his cup as his name was said, and Sabrina tipped her head at each one.

"Welcome, tutor Sabrina. How long have you been helping this sorry excuse for a baller?" the guy named Enrique asked. Gabe slapped his chest and guffawed heartily with the rest of them.

"Just this semester, so I've had a lot of work to do," she joked back, hoping humor would work. It did. The group cackled and fell over in their chairs.

"Oh, she's got your number, Reyes!" Enrique shouted.

"Nope. I got hers. Don't be jealous now."

More laughter, and the knot in Sabrina's chest loosened.

Tannis took her around the party, introducing her to so many people. *I'm never going to remember all of them, or their names,* she thought before Tannis shifted direction.

"Do you want a drink?"

His face was the epitome of happiness. Sabrina marveled at how this guy found joy in everything in life. Did nothing get him down?

"What are you drinking? I'll have that."

Tannis didn't answer. His eyes sparkled as he lowered his face. His cheeks were pink from something more than the heat when he looked at her again.

"Yeah. It's Sprite. With a few drops of apple juice."

Sabrina tried to peek into his cup. "What?"

His mesmerizing baby blues glanced up at the ceiling before returning to her.

"Yeah. I don't drink. So, I make a fake drink, carry it around, make sure my friends aren't too drunk to get home or stay here if they are wasted."

Diana's earlier words about stereotyping rang in her head.

"That's probably smart. Is there any diet Sprite?"

"You can drink if you want. I don't judge."

Sabrina bit her lip. "Yeah, but I don't drink that much either. In fact, I almost didn't come. Parties aren't exactly my scene."

Tannis dug in the fridge and uncovered a lone can of diet Sprite. He winked and poured it into a red cup.

"All about appearances," he asserted, handing it over. "Have you been to any parties this year?"

Sabrina shook her head, her silky tresses sticking to her cheek. She peeled them off. "Maybe three? Diana, my roommate, is a volleyball player, and she took me to a few.

Then some friends in the tutoring center had a big holiday blowout before winter break. None here at Damon's."

"Oh, you room with someone from the tall girl club. Nice. They get lots of invites. And they stick together. She seems like a good person to have your back. "

Sabrina nodded her head, not really focused on the conversation as much as she was on the fact that she'd talked to Tannis more in the past week than she had with nearly anyone else this semester. Including her ex.

For a player, Tannis sure came across as earnest and interested. Strike two against her stereotypes. And she hated herself a bit for having them. People stereotyped her all the time – and she reprimanded herself for falling into those very behaviors that she detested.

"She is. We've been friends since middle school."

"Yeah, same here with Damon."

"BRIN!" A loud voice called out, permeating the music and chatter, and Sabrina swung around. Diana stood with the tall girl from earlier and reached out to Sabrina.

"Come dance with us! You've been hiding from me all night!"

Sabrina shrugged at Tannis.

"I should make my rounds, say hi to a few more people. Have fun! Thanks for coming Sabrina. Maybe I'll get a dance in with you later tonight."

Then his tight body, clad in formfitting jeans and a black t-shirt, strolled off to the welcoming cheers of another group of partygoers, and the kitchen dimmed as the bright light Tannis carried with him left the room.

The party was a fun one, even for Sabrina. She felt more accepted than she had anticipated. Diana had told Sabrina she was worrying about nothing when she mentioned fitting in, and Diana had been right.

Diana's tall friend was named Chelle, and she had also been friendly the whole night. Chelle introduced Sabrina to a few other players on the MLC volleyball team as they danced, whose names she promptly forgot, and by the time she asked for directions to the bathroom, she was dripping with sweat.

Dim light flickered in the tight, cramped hallway which was crowded with people talking over the pounding clamor of music. The bathroom door was open, *thank God*.

When she opened the door to leave, a tall guy with brown, crew-cut style hair was right in the doorway. She jerked back, her heart leaping to her throat.

"Oh, sorry. I was getting ready to knock," he said.

His words sounded a bit slurred. and he reeked of beer. Not that it was strange. A lot of people at the party were well on their way to drunksville. Even Diana had imbibed her fair share.

"No problem. It's all yours."

Sabrina stepped to the side to move past the guy, but his arms draped against the door frame, and she'd have to walk under his stinking armpit to get by.

He's too drunk to stand.

"Excuse me," she offered, trying to squeeze past.

"No excuse necessary," he countered, leaning into her.

Sabrina tried to back up, only to have the counter ram into her backside.

This is not good, she thought. *This is very, very bad.*

"Hey, you gotta move so I can leave the bathroom." She hoped her voice sounded forceful so he might listen to her and get out of her way.

Maybe he was too drunk to realize he was blocking the door. She shifted, creeping to the doorway to squeeze past again.

"Hey, don't go anywhere too fast." His alcohol-laden breath was hot on her face, and she gagged. He chest bumped her, knocking her into the counter. *Chest bump! What the hell?*

The thickness in her throat grew into a solid ball, and she swallowed hard. *This is not good*, she thought once more. But there were people right there in the hall. Surely someone would see her predicament . . . drag this drunk guy away? *Anyone*?

He chest bumped her again, pushing her back into the bathroom a few inches, and Sabrina drew from a well of anger and self-preservation she didn't know she had. What she did know was this guy was hard core drunk and unsteady on his feet. In a rapid move, she planted her feet and shoved the guy's chest as hard as she could.

Sure enough, he was off-balance and stumbled backwards into the hall where the other partiers finally noticed something was wrong.

The drunk stood up and inhaled, puffing out his chest at Sabrina, but at least she was out of the cramped bathroom and in a public place. That ball in her throat shrunk, if a bit.

Then, before she could blink, the guy was on the ground on his back, and Tannis stood over him, one hand curled into the neckline of the guy's t-shirt, his other hand balled into a fist.

Any sign of Tannis's easy joviality was gone, replaced by hard lines and fury-burning eyes. The lean muscles of his arms, toned by years of ball-playing, erupted under his skin, strips of clenched power. This was not the nice, smiling Tannis from earlier, from English class, from tutoring. The smell of his burning anger overwhelmed the embedded smell of beer in the hallway.

"What the fuck, John! Damon told you to stay away from here! This is the last time. If you show up around us again, not only will I beat your ass into the ground, but Damon will have you fucking arrested. If he doesn't shoot you for trespassing!"

"Fuck you, Tan," the drunk John mumbled as he raised a weakened arm and grabbed Tannis's wrist at his neck. "You can't tell me what to do. "

"Oh, the fuck I can't."

A commotion in the hall caught Tannis's attention. He cocked his head at the noise. Rumbling, banging, a few short shrieks from some women – more than enough for Tannis to investigate. They'd had problems with drunk guys trying to punch each other, drunk girls getting into a frenzy or worse, drunk guys trying to mess with women they shouldn't. Damon, Tannis, their friends, and the rest of Tannis's baseball team, they didn't play that way. The unspoken rule was any troublemakers were immediately ejected and banned.

Tannis wove between the cluster of people, looking over their heads at the hall. Other partiers had formed a circle around the fighters, their eyes glued to the scene. Tannis peered over one short girl's blonde head.

He couldn't stop the grimace on his lips at the sight of John stumbling against the wall. *Fucking John.* Damon had thrown the guy out at the last party, physically picked him up and tossed him onto the driveway. A wall of ballplayers and other guys had stood as a wall behind Damon, ready to take up the mantle if John tried anything else.

From the way John cussed them out and flipped them off as he had stumbled down the sidewalk, Tannis thought he'd gotten the message that he was banned. Obviously not.

However, his disgust transformed into a black pit of fury when he shifted his gaze to the person he was fighting.

Or rather, the person who was defending herself against John.

Sabrina?

She stood like a tiny warrior in the doorway, legs spread apart and her dark eyes glittering as she stared down John. The image was so contrary to the quiet tutor he knew from the writing center, or the nervous person who had tried not to cry when her car battery died.

A defensive stance . . .

Tannis didn't hesitate. His mind faded to black. He clenched his jaw as he shoved past the blonde girl and jumped on top of John, grabbing at the man's neck. His fist balled up, ready to land a punch if the man so much as moved wrong.

"What the fuck, John! Damon told you last time to stay away from here! This is the last time. If you show up around us again, not only will I beat your ass into the ground, Damon will have you fucking arrested. If he doesn't shoot you for trespassing!"

"Fuck you, Tan," John spit at him. "You can't tell me what to do."

Tannis squeezed John's shirt harder, wrapping the fabric around his fist as his own muscles bulged.

"Oh, the fuck I can't."

With a powerful snap of his arm, the same move as winding up for a throw of the ball, Tannis lifted John half off the tile and dragged the drunk to the front door, ignoring the pathetic slapping at his hand. John was too drunk to even fight back.

Romeo stood at the door when Tannis reached it with the struggling John. With a grim smirk, Romeo opened the door and Tannis threw him out like yesterday's trash. John crumpled into a pile on the walkway. Tannis and Romeo remained at the door, chests heaving and fists ready for anything John might try next.

John rolled over, falling off the short step down, and groaned.

"Fuck you, Tannis. You're all fuckers," John managed, before he puked into the grass.

"Go home, John. Don't come back. Remember, you're banned from here!"

Romeo slammed the door, and Tannis spun around, racing back to the hallway.

"Sabrina!"

He found her with the rest of the curiously astonished crowd watching the drama unfold. Her roommate Diana had joined her and placed a protective arm around Sabrina's narrow shoulders. If nothing else, Damon always seemed to throw exciting parties, and who didn't love to watch a train wreck in action?

"Sabrina, you Ok?"

He thought she'd be in shock, and from her eyebrows riding high on her forehead, she was obviously feeling something like that. She crossed her arms over her chest as she tucked into Diana.

"Yeah," she said, blinking several times. "Yeah. He didn't want to let me out of the bathroom."

Tannis's chest threatened to explode at those words. Damon prided himself on having a house open to anyone who needed it, or just wanted to hang. A safe place. Damon's older brother was a cop for Christ's sake. And here was Sabrina's first time at one of these parties, and John tried an inappropriate move?

"Do you know that guy?" Diana asked. Tannis shook his head.

"Not really. He's an older guy, I'm not even sure he's a student. He came to a couple parties, was fun enough. But last time he was here, he got into a bloody fight. I don't even know what started it, but Damon broke it up, threw him out on his ass, and told him don't come back. He wasn't even supposed to be here. He's banned from Damon's house."

Tannis took one of Sabrina's hands, peeling it from her chest.

"Did he try something?"

The words got caught in this throat, choking him. The idea that he might have brought Sabrina to an unsafe place. . .

Every muscle in his body throbbed as his brain twisted what could have happened into a nightmare.

Sabrina shook her head and inhaled deeply.

"No. I don't know if he wanted to try something, or if he wanted to use the bathroom. He just wouldn't move."

"Until my girl made him move," Diana boasted. She squeezed her arm to hug Sabrina. "I didn't know how dangerous you are! You pack a wallop for such a shortie!"

A pinkish-bronze glow shaded Sabrina's skin, but she didn't pull away from Diana's hug or Tannis holding her hand.

"I had a little Krav Maga training when I was younger. Not much. And I sure as hell never expected to use it."

"So, you're good?" Diana asked. Sabrina nodded.

"Yeah, but I think I need to go home."

"Ok, I'll find Chelle and say goodbye."

Tannis's lips thinned briefly before he forced his wide smile back on his face. He'd wanted to spend more time with Sabrina, to get the chance to talk with her, but that hadn't worked out.

"Do you need me to drive you home?" he asked.

Sabrina raised her eyes to him, the deep black like the night sky, impossibly dark and never ending, sucking him in.

Those eyes, that was the first thing he'd noticed about her when he met her the first day of class. Her eyes never stopped searching, investigating, studying the world with an unending intensity. And when her eyes landed on him, they caught him in a trap, holding him, and his heart had stopped.

No one had ever looked at him that way, with eyes that gripped and held on as he fell farther into those midnight depths. Her eyes held the whole universe. He forgot who he

41

was, where he was, what he was doing when she'd turned that brilliant black gaze on him, until Enrique elbowed him to bring him back to the light.

She spoke, and Tannis missed it. *Pay attention, Reyes!*

"I'm sorry. What?"

"I didn't drink, so I'm ok to drive."

Damn. There goes driving her home.

"Can I at least walk you to your car?"

Had he ever been so consumed by someone before? The longer he was around her, the more he longed to know her. Unlike most of his other friends – loud, outgoing, wild – Sabrina was contained, focused. She was a cryptic secret he wanted to learn.

Though he couldn't say it, he thought everything he was feeling about Sabrina was plain on his face.

A slap to the back of his head interrupted his thoughts.

"Way to introduce Sabrina to our parties, Reyes. You'll be lucky if she ever wants to see us again."

Damon had a way of bringing Tannis back to himself, providing a moment of relief, and Tannis's slick smile beamed at the shorter, stockier man.

"No, she probably never wants to see *you* again. I have tutoring with her over the summer, so she's stuck with me."

Diana's lean form caught the corner of his eye.

"Here comes Diana. Let me walk you out," he told Sabrina.

Tannis opened the door and left it open as he walked Sabrina outside. Diana and Chelle followed them out, keeping a distance. *Ahh, Diana's the best kind of friend*, Tannis thought, *a wing-woman.*

"I'm so sorry that you had someone threaten you like that. I feel like it's my fault for that guy being here."

"Hey," Sabrina swung her head so her sleek hair poured over her bright white blouse. "You didn't invite the guy. You don't know the guy. Damon even banned him. I don't blame you. And nothing happened. With how he puked on the grass when he landed outside, he probably was just looking for the toilet."

"Thank you for that. And either way, his behavior was out of line. Hopefully, he got the message this time."

Too soon, they were at her car. He reached for the driver's door to open it for her, his heart racing in his chest.

He'd planned on asking her out, but her roommate was *right there*. The party didn't go as planned, and never had Tannis felt more like an embarrassed middle schooler in his life. The question wouldn't pass his lips.

"Ask her already!" Diana shouted from behind him. Tannis dropped his gaze as his cheeks burned, and his smile transformed into an embarrassed pinch of his lips. For a man who just throttled another man in front of a large group of onlookers, Tannis was shocked at his own hesitation.

Sabrina paused getting into her car.

"Ask me what?"

Tannis lifted his face. "I'm normally so much smoother than this. But, can we get together sometime this week? Not for tutoring?"

Sabrina's dark eyes narrowed.

"Not for tutoring?" She paused, drawing out his misery, then shocked him with a slight smile. "I need to study for finals tomorrow, but most of my exams are done by Wednesday. I tutor until six. Want to meet up after that?"

"I'm done at six, too. I'll text you for details?"

"That sounds like a plan."

Tannis's languid grin returned, and he closed her door as she settled behind the wheel. Diana paused and winked at him before folding her long frame into the passenger side. He knocked on the roof and stepped back as the car pulled away.

"Shit," Chelle said, and he jerked his head to the volleyballer standing on the broken sidewalk. "Took you long enough. You must really like her."

She wasn't wrong. He shot her a grin and thrust out his elbow to escort her back to the party. "Shut it, Chelle. Want to head back?"

Chapter Four

A DRUNKEN DIANA joked and teased Sabrina about Tannis the whole drive home. She kept saying "He was gonna beat the shit out of that guy for you!" in an intoxicated slur, then she crashed into bed once they were in the apartment. Sabrina had blushed sheepishly at her comments, particularly when she'd told Sabrina the blond baller had deserved at least a kiss for defending her honor. Secretly, Sabrina liked the teasing and had a somber moment of sadness that Diana was going to be gone all summer.

Sabrina woke early on Sunday, made a gigantic pot of cheap coffee, and locked herself in her room to study. Finals week meant four finals, and though she was confident about two of them, the remaining two were shockingly comprehensive as evidenced by the online study guides. Sabrina had to make sure she nailed them.

That 3.8 GPA number danced before her like a ghost, a specter that haunted her. To keep her scholarships, Sabrina needed to hit that number. She surrounded herself with textbooks and papers and highlighters, with her laptop sitting on its throne over all of it. A vortex of review material. She wrapped her silky hair in a loose bun with a scrunchie and buckled down.

Poor Diana had to pack *and* study. She was set to leave the weekend right after finals. That thought was another phantom haunting Sabrina. Now Sabrina was going to have to make up that difference in rent, and she'd be lonely those three months over summer. Unlike many people, Sabrina was fond of her roommate. She shoved those thoughts aside to focus on her notes.

Late in the day, she picked up her phone to check messages. One missed text from Adele. While in her hand, her phone dinged. Expecting it to be Diana asking if she wanted dinner (she was also going to miss having a wife – Sabrina hated thinking about dinner!), she tapped the screen to read the text.

It was from Tannis.

-- *Checking in and seeing how studying was going.*

Her finger was poised to text back right away.

But she didn't.

Is this a stupid idea? she asked herself. *The athlete and the brain? Wasn't that the plot for every bad 80s movie?*

Diana didn't think so, and her opinion went far with Sabrina. And in Sabrina's head, she had another thought with that one – Tannis wasn't like any other athlete she'd met or tutored.

Now that sounded like a line from a movie!

He wasn't like anyone else, though. Tannis was, well, *nice.* For all he was ready to beat the shit out of the drunk from the night before, Tannis was a nice guy. It seemed like a generic description, but it fit. He had friends from every walk of life, not just ball players. He didn't tease or mock others.

Did it matter if he was a jock and she wasn't? Could a relationship with him work out?

You're not marrying him, she reminded herself. *It's just a date.*

It wasn't like they were in high school anymore. And Diana was going to be gone for the summer. Jana was going to be back home as well. Adele planned on staying with her roommates, but working, not taking a class, and Sabrina didn't know how much she might see her.

It'd be nice to be dating someone. Maybe not be as lonely.

Even if he just ended up a friend.

Tannis's nice guy status won out. She texted him back, giving him a summary of her day and asked about his.

-- *We still tutoring on Wednesday?* he texted.

-- *Our regular time? You won't have any more English classes, so I didn't think so.*

-- *So tutoring won't start again until summer classes begin?*

Why all the questions about tutoring? Her skin blazed and her brain was on fire. Too much was happening for her to focus. Did she misinterpret his question last night about meeting up? It wasn't a date? It was tutoring he was asking about?

She dropped her head back on her chair and closed her eyes.

What a fool she'd been. Of course, the jock didn't want to date the tutor. That only happened in bad 80s movies.

Sabrina blinked rapidly. *I'm not crying.* Why would she be crying? He was just a tutoring student after all, an acquaintance at best.

Gritting her teeth, she inhaled deeply and tried to answer the text in a way that didn't sound like she'd been stupid enough to think it was a date.

--Yeah, in two weeks. If your schedule changes, let me know.

There, that sounded like a tutor response, not an "I thought this was a date" response.

Her phone dinged.

--Two weeks? I can't wait that long. It's a good thing we are going out on Wednesday night.

Then a smiley face.

Wait, so it is a date?

One thing Sabrina had learned with her writing was to take chances. Stronger writing came from a difference, an unexpected aspect to the paper, the essay, the response. Risk-taking wasn't her strong suit in real life. Sabrina was the type who played everything safe, except in her writing.

Maybe it was time to apply risk-taking to real life.

She licked her lips and hovered her thumb over her phone.

--*Where are we going Wednesday night?*

Three dots blinking . . .

--*I'm working on it. What do you like to do?*

Not parties, she thought. But if she gave him her list, he might balk.

--*Movies.*

--*That's it? Movies? come on . . .*

Sabrina set her phone on her desk and stared at her notes in front of her.

He asked . . .

She grabbed a scrunchy from the edge of her desk and added it to her floppy, messy bun that was falling off the top of her head.

Time to take this to the next level. *Let's see just how into me he is.* Her next text was pure honesty.

-- *Museums. Art shows. Book signings. Music in the park. Shakespeare in the park. Coffee houses.*

She set her phone back down and waited for him to get over his shock. Stereotyping was horrible, but a heady sense of certainty settled in her chest that he'd not done many, if any, of the events she listed.

--*What is Shakespeare in the park?*

That response she wasn't ready for. She'd assumed he'd go for the coffee house.

--*A Shakespeare play, but outside. You bring a picnic blanket and food and stuff. They do it at Salamander Park on weekend afternoons during the summer.*

Three dots . . .

--Favorite coffee house?

--The beanery.

--Ok, gotta go!

What? That was abrupt!

-- Bye!

What else was she going to say? At least it's going to be a date . . . a real date.

She set the phone on her desk and returned to her stacks of notes. Her mind wouldn't focus, and the words in her notebook kept shifting and dancing. She peeked into her coffee cup and found nothing but weak dregs.

Plus, it was getting late. An over-caffeinated Sabrina wouldn't sleep well and would mean disaster for her eight a.m. final. She'd grab dinner with Diana, text Adele back, and ponder her potential date with Tannis later.

"So Tannis, are you going out with that Sabrina? She doesn't seem your type." Ken whipped a fastball that threw up dust from Tannis's glove when it hit the pocket.

"Yeah. I like her. She's more than just *a type.* Something about her. Why? Were you gonna ask her out?"

Ken's lips thrust forward as he readied for Tannis's return throw.

"Nope. Just, there's a lot of women in the pond. Seems an odd one to go for."

Tannis had cupped the ball in his glove but stopped and stood ramrod straight. *An odd one?*

"What's that mean, Xiao?"

Ken dropped his glove to his hip. "She's a mousy tutor. She obviously doesn't like to party, as we saw the other night. I just don't think she's the right fit for someone like you."

Blood hammered in Tannis's temples. He stared daggers at Ken.

"Who the fuck are you to say something like that? You're going to insult who I want to date? Do I go around saying you're a short guy who sucks at throwing a curve? No, because I don't talk like that about people. And I like her. You shitting on that isn't going to change my mind."

Ken's face darkened, his eyes narrowing at Tannis as he took a step forward.

"I was just saying. You're an ass, Tannis."

With a sudden ferocious and unexplainable heat, Tannis threw his glove on the ground and rushed Ken, his face eclipsing the shorter pitcher.

"I'm not the one who started his day by insulting someone who probably worked just as hard or harder to get in this school. The one who decided he's somehow better because he's on the baseball team but struggling to pass his psych class."

"Get the fuck away, Tannis," Ken growled and slammed his hands into Tannis's chest. His lean frame barely shifted with the force of Ken's push.

"You don't want to put hands on me, Ken. I didn't have to beat the shit out of John, but that doesn't mean I won't beat the shit out of you."

"I'd like to see you try." Ken shoved him again.

This time Tannis was prepared and only one of Ken's hands caught his shoulder. Ken stumbled off balance when his other hand didn't land, and Tannis spun to kick Ken's upright ass. Ken spilled into the dirt that puffed around him.

In a flash, Ken was back on his feet, grabbing at Tannis's uniform, and gritting his teeth, Tannis pressed his hand against Ken's face, twisting him away.

"Break it up! Right now!"

Coach's voice carried over the diamond, and a pair of hands grabbed Tannis around his shoulders, pulling him from Ken. Coach Alzugaray had leapt behind Ken, wrapping him in a bear like grip so his hands yanked off Tannis.

"What is wrong with the two of you?" Coach Garcia stood between them, hands on his hips and eyes blazing. "We have our final game this Friday, and you two are fighting? What the hell kind of teamwork is this?"

Ken thrust his arm forward to break free from Coach Alzugaray. He spit on the ground before sending a hateful glare to Tannis, who stood panting, his chest shuddering with each breath that passed from his lungs.

"Ok, Xiao, you run laps around the bases. Tannis, you run around the outside of the bleachers. I'll deal with each of you in a minute."

They didn't move until Coach shoved each off in their own directions.

Tempting

Tannis scuffed his feet against the dirt as he jogged to the bleachers. His brain was on fire, droplets of sweat rolling from his hairline to the vee of his practice uniform. And his confusion over Ken's reaction made his head burn more.

What the hell was wrong with Ken? Why did he react so badly to Sabrina? Was he jealous because his grades were slipping and she was really smart? Or did he really have a superiority complex? Were they back in high school, each clique hating another?

Tannis picked up his pace, reminiscing about high school and how he hadn't belonged to one group there either. He brought that behavior to college, and truly believed that, now as adults, people would behave better, be more open to those different from them. Maybe he'd been very wrong.

His pace steadily increased as his arms pumped by his side. Breathe in, breathe out. Step, step. He'd seen evidence that people stuck to their own on campus, particularly with athletes since he spent so much time with them.

Tannis hated that *stuck* perspective and wondered why people did that – formed arbitrary cliques. Obviously, similar interests didn't mean likability, as evidenced by his interaction with Ken.

A pair of jogging footfalls patted along his right side, and Tannis broke from his thoughts to see Enrique jogging next to him, his shiny black hair almost blue under his cap. He said nothing – he just jogged. Romeo soon joined them, then two more players from his team. They said nothing, running with him in solidarity. That moment of his teammates running laps with him – he would remember it for the rest of his life.

Between the run and his teammates joining him, the hard knot in his chest loosened, unraveled enough that his clenched muscles relaxed.

The fire burning in Tannis's mind cooled as well. At least he wasn't the only one who felt this way about Ken's idea of sticking to one's own type.

They rounded the curve of the bleachers to find Coach standing like a statue, legs spread and arms crossed over his gigantic chest. His face was a mask — Tannis couldn't tell how pissed Coach was but assumed it was bad. *What else could it be?*

The group of men slowed their pace. Enrique pounded Tannis's back, told him "Good luck," in a low voice, and they took off to the lockers to change.

"Come sit on the bleachers with me Tannis."

Coach Garcia perched on the edge of the metal bench and rested his elbows on his knees. Tannis sat a few feet away and hung his head to his chest.

"You've been on the team with Xiao for a year. I've never had any problem with you. You've been my poster boy. If you have any trouble fighting, I haven't seen it. What's going on?"

Tannis rubbed his sweaty, gritty face with his hands. He pulled off his cap, swept his damp hair off his head, and replaced it, never once lifting his eyes to Coach.

"I don't get into fights, coach. Not much. I mean, if something gets out of hand or I need to back someone up . . ."

"That's not what I'm talking about, Reyes. Xiao is a teammate. Try again."

Tannis rubbed his eyes.

54

"So, Ok. I don't know how to explain it, but remember when you were in high school, and the tweakers didn't hang out with the jocks, the jocks didn't hang out with drama geeks, they didn't hang with the brainiacs . . ."

Coach sat up, resting his hand on his knee. "Yeah? Like, high school cliques. John Hughes movie style?"

A thin bubble of laughter caught in Tannis's chest.

"Yeah, like that. In college, we've gotten away from that, new place, new people and all. But over this year, some people fell back into those patterns. Right? I didn't. I mean, I've always had friends from all over. But Ken, he – " Tannis flicked his eyes at Coach who looked down his nose with his face scrunched in confusion.

"You got in a fight because you were reliving a bad teen movie?" Coach's voice was tight, disbelieving.

"No, not just that. But I know this girl – "

"Ahh," Coach sat back, shifting his elbows to rest them on the bleacher behind him. "There it is. You got into a fight over a girl."

Testosterone at its finest. Tannis shook his head because that wasn't quite accurate.

"No, not just a girl. Ken thinks I can do better, and he was talking shit about her."

The knowing expression on Coach's face slipped. "What do you mean, better?"

"That's what I said!" Tannis sat up tall, poking a finger at his chest. Finally, Coach was getting it. "He thinks that Sabrina – Sabrina Alonto, she's my tutor – is not, well, right, for a ball player. He was a real dick about it."

Coach rolled his eyes and pursed his lips.

"How bad?"

"What?"

"How bad was the comment? It had to be pretty bad for you to lose it. You might have a fiery temper and are fast with your fists, but you're also a slow burn. I've yet to see it until today. So, it must have been pretty bad. Or did someone else start saying something, and Ken just topped it off?"

"No, no one but Ken. More than just what he said, but how he said it, you know?"

Coach nodded, keeping his laser sharp gaze on Tannis.

"Who threw the first punch?"

Tannis rubbed his hand on the back of his neck. The pounding in his temples returned.

"No punches really. He insulted Sabrina. I insulted him back. We cursed, and he pushed me. Tried again and I moved, kicked him in the ass. That's about all that happened when you found us."

Coach was quiet, staring into the horizon. Tannis waited, the heaviness of the moment pressing against his chest like one of the giant Stonehenge blocks. He picked at his stained pants as he waited for Coach to speak again.

"This reads like a bad teen movie, that is for certain. Nice classicism going on to boot. Is it serious with this girl? I've not seen you serious about anyone since you got to MLC."

Tannis dipped his eyes. "No, she's my tutor – "

Coach gave a low, whistling exhale.

"I know," Tannis continued. "I met her in English class. I needed help, you know, to keep my scholarship, and she's nice. That's the start. But the more I worked with her, we started talking. Last week her car broke down. And I was able to help her get it going, one thing led to another —"

"Whoa —" Coach exclaimed. Tannis held up a hand.

"No, no, one thing led to another, and I invited her to a party, lots of people. Her roommate is Diana, on the volleyball team? So she came. Sabrina fit right in and we had fun. A drunk guy ruined it, so we kicked him out. I texted her this weekend, trying to figure out a great first date . . ."

One of Coach's bushy eyebrows rose in a questioning arch. "You got into a fight with Ken over a girl you haven't even taken out on a date yet?"

Tannis's cheeks burned. "I guess, but it was more Ken's elitist attitude I had a problem with."

"What are you going to do now?"

"About what? Ken?"

"Well, yeah, and the tutor. Are you still going to date her? Or did Ken's insults change your mind?"

"What? No? I don't care what Ken thinks."

Coach leaned forward on his knees again, his face even with Tannis's.

"You don't care what anyone thinks, Tannis. That sounds like a bad thing, but it's a good thing. It means you are willing to take chances. We always say that you miss one hundred percent of the shots you don't take. And you, Tannis, are willing to take them all. Don't let people like Ken get to you. And next time, let him have his say, and just bow out. Don't let him drag you into trouble. You guys are teammates, after all."

Tannis bounced his legs, tapping his heel against the metal bleachers.

Tempting

"How much trouble am I in?" he finally asked.

Coach sat up tall again and stared him down. His face didn't shift as he rubbed the bridge of his nose.

"Extra laps tomorrow and Wednesday. Wipe the lockers down. Be grateful I don't make you clean the toilets and sit out the first inning at Friday's game."

Tannis's chin fell to his chest.

"Got it?" Coach's words were angry, but his tone wasn't. Tannis knew he wanted his team to be the best they could be, and Tannis hadn't been that person today.

"Got it. Thanks, Coach."

Coach slapped his hand on Tannis's back, letting it rest there for a moment before rising and leaving Tannis to contemplate on the bleachers.

Tannis let Coach's advice roll around in his head. The team had left the field, so it was quiet, just Tannis, the tweeting birds, and the low rumble of distant cars on the highway. He got off light, he knew. And coach was right – he shouldn't have let Ken get to him. He never had before, and it wasn't the first time Ken or his cronies made off comments about others.

Running footsteps sounded behind him, and Tannis turned around to see Coach coming back.

"Here." Coach pulled two pieces of paper from his sweats pocket and extended them to Tannis.

"What are these?" Tannis asked, taking them and turning them over. He flicked his eyes to Coach. "Rocky's?"

"Mini golf. Great first date. A bit of fun competition, you can talk the whole time, you aren't alone if it's not going well. You can eat after if it is. I got some promo stuff from a few local vendors, and I've been sitting on those for a while."

58

Tannis slapped the passes against his palm. His tight cheeks relaxed, a hint of his smile returning. "Thanks, Coach."

"Now head back to the lockers, change, and text Sabrina and let her know when you'll be there."

Tempting

Chapter Five

MINI-GOLF? AT FIRST, Sabrina thought he must be joking. *Seriously? Mini-golf?* The last time she'd played miniature golf she had been, what, twelve? With her family?

But she beat him by four, even though they stopped keeping track after the sixth hole – the windmill. It hadn't helped him that Tannis stood by the panels and extended his sinewy arms to hold them in place, allowing her ball to roll into the hole-in-one opening.

"That's totally cheating," she'd called out.

"Um, since it's helping you, I'm not sure how that works!"

61

That smile. He was all tan and dimples and lips and joy, and she sucked in several sharp breaths each time he flashed that smile at her.

After she won, they returned their clubs to the counter, and he took her to the food court where they celebrated with melty mozzarella sticks and sodas.

"Well, I'm not sure how you came up with this idea, but it's a hell of a lot better than a bar. Or a movie."

Tannis sipped his soda. "Well, Shakespeare in the park doesn't happen until this weekend, and I wasn't sure coffee counted as a date."

Date. The word sent a shiver up her spine. How had a short writing tutor ended up on a date with the most desirable man on campus? Everything about him exuded a lazy sultriness – even the way his full lips wrapped around that straw. And sucked . . .

Her stomach quivered and a rush of heat flooded her entire body. *Focus, Sabrina.*

"Then this was a good choice. I haven't been to mini-golf in ages."

"Neither have I. It was more fun that I thought it would be," he admitted.

His alluring lips curled, and his smile transformed from easy to seductive. Sabrina crossed her legs under the table. She was certain her panties would fly off the longer she stared at him. Tannis lifted his piercing eyes that caught hers in a liquid gaze. He looked so tempting sitting across from her, that she could lose all control.

"Or, maybe it was the company," his velvety voice added.

Tempting

Her mind was still trying to wrap itself around his words when Tannis reached across the dark wood table. He skimmed his warm fingertip across her hand, and like a live wire, her skin sizzled, electrified under his touch. All the air rushed out of her lungs, leaving her ragged and panting and waiting, waiting to see what this electric touch would lead to.

Planting his other hand on the table, Tannis lifted himself from the seat and bent into her. He supported himself on one arm, his muscles bulging under his shirtsleeves as she unthinkingly drifted closer. Sabrina had to lift her face to his, and each breath she took was a slow, steady pant. She froze under his gaze, her lips parting without her knowledge or permission, waiting for the impossible, for his lips to touch hers with the same electricity as his finger.

With shocking slowness, Tannis pressed into her, and his full lips claimed just her lower lip. He brushed his lips against her bottom lip, a gentle sweep that made her thighs quiver. His kiss on that one lip became more aggressive, licking then biting. His teeth bit hard enough into her lip to pull it forward before his tongue slipped over her mouth to her upper lip. He stroked, licked, and sucked so gently every nerve ending was on fire – her toes, her ears, her fingertips.

Her hands clenched at the table, her knuckles white with exertion. Her nipples went hard, and her pussy dripped with need, with want, with an unabiding craving she hadn't thought possible.

Her entire world shifted on its axis. Sabrina was willing to give up everything for that one kiss.

One single kiss.

A kiss that didn't even touch both lips at the same time.

Then Tannis withdrew, retaking his seat, and he bit his lower lip in a smoldering smile. Sabrina touched her lips, wondering if she could still feel anything after that single moment, a series of feeling and sensations that she hadn't known could exist.

All from one kiss.

"Was that too soon? Too much?" he asked.

Sabrina couldn't speak. She had no air in her shaky lungs.

The kiss was a bold move, but seeing her sitting there across the table, stabbing at her drink with her straw and her lips curving around her appetizer, mesmerized him. Then her lips glistened with the residual oil, begging to be licked. So he licked.

Tannis's blood boiled hot throughout his body when he pulled away. The only thing that stopped him from throwing her on the table and satisfying that burning need in his groin was the fact that several families were in the same room. He would have killed for a bed, a couch, the back seat of his car . . .

"And we got that whole, first kiss awkwardness over," he told her as he grabbed a cheese stick.

Though he might have appeared calm on the outside, his heart wanted to burst in his chest at his bold move. Tannis hadn't had a real girlfriend since high school, and even then, he hadn't thought himself ready for anything serious, so those relationships didn't last long. Over the past year, since he went from woman to woman, he'd acquired a bit of a reputation as a player, and not just a ball player.

But he hadn't had sex in months. Moving from one girl to the next was a way to keep teammates and overly curious gossips busy, including Damon, the most nosy of them all. Or they wanted to set him up with someone. If his friends thought he was a player, well, no one wanted a guy like that dating their sister, or even their sister's best friend. It was perfect.

Until Sabrina.

At first, he had considered a casual date or two, to try hanging out with someone beyond his normal circle of friends. Maybe that was the problem.

Then he spent more time with her, in English class, at tutoring, and the last thing he wanted was for her to be just another quick date to keep his reputation intact.

Her hair, usually pulled to the side over her shoulder, was so smooth, so shiny, like black silk. And her eyes – they had an intensity behind them, as though she studied every detail of everything in her view. She was a serious student; she didn't smile much. She might have thought him a class clown because she didn't know he was doing it all to see those beautifully petulant lips fight themselves into a smile.

He'd been dreaming of those lips.

His next problem had been, how to ask her out?

Most of his dates were casual, at a party or hanging out with friends, a quick question, and move on.

Sometimes the universe worked in his favor. What were the odds that her car would break down right there when he was parked nearby?

Tannis dipped his head to his straw and smiled to himself.

Such amazing odds.

"No," Sabrina said with a sigh, "not too much. Not too soon."

"Does this mean you are up for a second date? Maybe we could try that Shakespeare thing this weekend?"

Her rounded cheeks sucked in. "Why would you want to go to Shakespeare in the park? It doesn't seem like your thing."

"You think I can't appreciate Shakespeare?"

Sabrina cocked her head, studying him with her watchful gaze. Like a wild cat surveying her prey.

"Name one play other than Romeo and Juliet that you read in high school."

Tannis leaned back on the bench, lifting his thumb to his lip, and met her gaze.

"That one, the old Mel Gibson film. Where he was mad at his mom?"

One side of Sabrina's lips curled upward. "Keep going."

Tannis flung his head backward, shaking out his tawny locks. "Uhh. Ok, he dies at the end, in a sword fight or something."

Sabrina crossed her arms over her wonderful breasts, and Tannis forced his eyes to stay on her smile.

"And the title?"

This time, her eyebrow flinched when he licked his lip. The title of the film was slippery, like a broken egg and he was trying to hold the yolk. The title was one word . . . And it was like a food? Chicken? Beef? Ham –

"Hamlet! Mel Gibson was Hamlet!"

Sabrina's jaw didn't fully drop, but it shifted into an open-mouth smile that nearly knocked him off his seat.

"I won't say I'm shocked, because that might sound insulting, but I'm tripping out that you could name one."

"Is that a yes?"

"A yes?"

"To Shakespeare in the Park this weekend? Finals are over. I have my last game out in Orange County on Friday, and summer classes don't start for a week after that. We can make it a picnic."

"Do you know what play is this weekend?" Her question was pure velvet. Almost a purr.

His hand slipped to his chest as he barked out a laugh.

"No idea. I don't even know what time it starts."

"A Midsummer Night's Dream. You can meet Puck. And it starts at two."

Tannis leaned over the table again, grasping her hands.

"So, it's a date?"

Sabrina's intense eyes narrowed, crinkling at the corners. "Yes, a second date."

Tannis winked at her. "Who's Puck?"

67

Tempting

Chapter Six

"CHELLE SAID SHE saw you at Mini-Golf with that girl you invited to the party."

Damon grabbed a blue and white beer can from the fridge. He didn't offer one to Tannis. He knew better.

"Sabrina. Yeah, we had a good time."

"You bang her yet?"

Tannis rolled his eyes. "Come on, Damon."

One glossy black eyebrow rose on Damon's forehead. "A second date?"

Tannis's cheeks heated and he coughed into his fist to hide his blush.

"Yeah, a second date."

Tempting

Damon popped the top of the can, a fizzy burst of beer drops spraying them both. He sucked down a swig, then eyed Tannis.

"You don't do second dates," he deadpanned.

Tannis didn't say anything. He knew what a second date meant. So did Damon.

"Dude, I'm not going to say anything, but you know you're gonna get slack for that. She's not quite, well, your type?"

"My type?" Tannis shook his head. "What the hell does that mean? I date all types."

"Not *this* type. She's super smart, right? Not an athlete. Not a partier?"

"She's great friends with Diana, who is both of those, so that says something. She's not a boring schoolmarm or whatever you're thinking. And I don't imagine much slack. It's ridiculous to think that."

Damon held up his beer can like a shield. "Hey man. I don't care. Hell, you're friends with me and I keep dropping out of school. I'm a gear head. I know the real you. But those guys out there? Especially ball players and their groupies?" Damon flicked his head like he was pointing at the campus. "They may not. And if there's one thing I've learned, it's that people like to stick to their own. Some of your friends might look down on this thing with your tutor."

Tannis pressed his hand against the counter to hold himself still and tone down the throbbing in his chest. His teeth clenched together as he spoke.

"Unlike some of those people you're talking about, I'm not a judgmental fuck."

Damon held up his hands. "Hey, that's not me, dude. Like I said, I don't care. You do you. Whatever makes you happy, and if she makes you happy, then I am all for it. But people won't like her because she's different. She's smart, and they aren't. So, jealousy. She's focused on her education, her future, and they aren't. She doesn't dress like them, talk like them. She'll be a target, in any way they can make it, if they feel threatened. It's what people do, my brother. Just be ready for it when it happens and decide if she's worth fighting for. Because with some of these shit heads we know, it might come to that."

Damon tipped the can to his lips as Tannis rubbed his mouth with the palm of his hand.

"You ever think of becoming like one of those life coaches? Or a speaker. You always thought too deep for your own good."

Damon's wry grin was infectious. He belched.

"I know, right?"

Diana brushed a loose lock of hair that escaped from her braid off her forehead. Sabrina's hair managed to stay tight in her high ponytail, but it didn't stop the sweat that coated her everywhere. Why did Diana have to move on the hottest day of spring?

"At least this is the last box," Diana said as she slammed down her trunk. "My dad already got my bed and dresser, and the rest will just stay. If you do have a roommate or a visitor, they can use whatever they want of my stuff in the room."

Sabrina wiped her sopping brow with the bottom of her t-shirt.

"Sounds like a plan. But I don't exactly have out of town guests scheduled."

Diana lunged at Sabrina and wrapped her in a tight hug. It was easy for Sabrina to forget how tall and strong Diana was, but her hugs like this one were ready reminders. Sabrina felt like a kid when Diana hugged her.

"And here," Diana pulled away and reached into her back pocket. She held out several green bills. "Another hundred. That's about all I can help you with for June. Is that Ok?"

Sabrina took the money and shoved it into the pocket of her shorts. "Yeah. I spoke to the manager after finals on Thursday. He said he can reduce my rent by two hundred a month for three months, then we just need to pay an extra $50 for the rest of the year to make up for it."

"Well, I'll make sure my financial aid knows about the extra fifty to get them to pay for it in the fall."

Sabrina's shoulders dropped with relief. "That's good. That should work out perfect. This two hundred makes it even for June, then whatever you can do for July and August. Either way, I'm just glad this all worked out."

Diana had leaned against her car, and Sabrina did the same. Her roommate didn't seem to be in a big rush to leave.

"It's three months, not even that if you move back before the end of August," Sabrina told her. Diana must have had something on her mind. Not leaving right away suggested she wanted to talk to Sabrina.

"So, you have another date with Tannis this weekend?" Diana's full lips tightened into a slight smile. Not a warm smile. Sabrina stiffened, on edge.

"Yeah. He's taking me to Shakespeare in the Park. We're doing a picnic or something."

Diana didn't look at Sabrina, her eyes focused on the distant view.

"Tannis is a great guy, don't get me wrong, Sabrina, and he seems really into you. In a way I don't think anyone's seen before, which makes me excited. But he's not known for his dating record, you know what I mean?"

Diana's deep blue eye's flicked to Sabrina then back to the horizon. Sabrina nodded. She reached for her ponytail and pulled the smooth length through her fingers.

"Yeah. He's not the dating type. I don't hang with your crowd, Diana, and even I knew that."

"I'm not saying he's just out for a good time. When I saw him with you at the party, and some gossip I've been hearing, he seems to like you. A lot. That's the other problem. The one you just mentioned. And it pisses me off."

Sabrina dropped her ponytail and turned to Diana. "What problem I mentioned?"

Diana dropped her gaze to her white Nikes and kicked her toe against the asphalt.

"Some athletes and those who hang in that crowd can be very clique-ish. Totally high school. Or worse – like middle school. And people don't like that Tannis is interested in you. They think he should stick with someone who's more . . . "

Sabrina didn't need her to finish. "Athletic. Taller. More traditionally attractive. Less book-smart?"

Diana's beautiful lips pulled down as Sabrina spoke.

"I didn't tell you this, but Chelle and I had to get into Gabe's face this week. He was talking shit about Tannis bringing you to the party and told me to 'talk to my girl.' You can imagine how that went over, especially with Chelle there. She's big into anti-bullying. I guess she was bullied a lot before she hit her growth spurt and started playing volleyball. I had to pull her away and we basically told Gabe to stick it."

Sabrina licked her suddenly dry lips. This did sound like a bad 80s romance! If she hadn't been so insulted, so distressed, she might have laughed.

"Thank you for sticking up for me."   She didn't know what else to say.

Diana's eyes narrowed. "People like that, they don't know what they're saying. They're stuck in a way of thinking that's so juvenile. We're adults now, not dumb high schoolers. We're going to meet all sorts of people in college, in work, in life, and it says something if we try to put people into little boxes."

Then Diana's blue gaze softened, and she took Sabrina's hand. "You are one of my best friends, Sabrina. And if I'd thought the same way, that never would have happened. I would have been stuck in my box and you in yours. We're better than that. I think Tannis is better than that, too. And until these ass-hats figure it out, you might have to put on a tough skin if they say anything to you. Is it worth it?"

Sabrina's head snapped back.

"Is what worth it?"

74

"Tannis, the possibility of dating him, maybe having a real relationship with him. Is it worth it?"

Sabrina let her eyes wander out to the horizon where Diana had been staring. *Tannis's smile? That kiss? His eager, happy attitude? Oh yes. And it's all just fun, right? Nothing too serious. Is it worth the risk?*

"Yeah. I've got tough skin. We all do. It's worth it."

Tempting

Chapter Seven

THE SUN STILL hung high in the sky, covering the park in a blanket of blindingly bright light and chest-clenching heat.

But that heat was nothing compared to the burning low in Sabrina's abdomen when Tannis threaded his arm through hers and led her to a clear space in the park near the wooden stage. The baseball team had won their last game of the season, and Tannis walked like he was king of the world. Or at least, king of MLC.

He carried a basket – an actual picnic basket! – in his left arm. After he set it down, he pulled the cloth off the top and flipped it out into its full blanket size and let it billow onto the grass. Sabrina clapped at his dramatic flair and settled onto the blanket.

"I can't buy wine legally yet, so it's a bottle of diet Sprite," he admitted as he lifted the green plastic bottle from the basket. "And I didn't know what food to bring to something like this. But it's fancy, so I got what I thought was fancy food."

Sabrina bit her lower lip as a giggle bubbled in her throat. Tannis put such effort into this date, and she wasn't about to make him think she was mocking him. Biting back that laugh was even more difficult as he placed a container of hummus, a baggie of carrots, a pack of crackers, a bag of cubed cheese, and a package of summer sausage on the blanket. Then he swept his hands over it like he was a game-show host displaying the prize.

She couldn't handle it anymore. She burst out laughing and clapped her hands again.

Tannis tore into the packages and created several snack stacks, offering them to Sabrina. He poured the Sprite into two clear plastic cups and offered one to her. Tannis held his cup up.

"A toast?"

Sabrina tapped her cup against his.

"A toast to what?"

"To us. To the start of something wonderful."

Sabrina's heated blush added to the heat of the day, and she was certain she would explode from the smoldering heat. She sipped her Sprite and set it to the side.

They ate melty cheese and crackers as the play began. Sabrina didn't watch the play as much as her eyes wandered to Tannis to see how he liked the performance. He stayed interested in the first few scenes, but it was obvious his attention started to drift by the start of Act Two.

At least he wasn't scrolling through his phone.

"We can leave," she said suddenly. Tannis blinked rapidly and faced her.

"What? Why?"

"I know Shakespeare isn't everyone's favorite. If you're bored, we can go."

His dancing azure eyes remained fixed on hers.

"Hell, no. I want to see what else this Puck guy does. He's a riot."

He reached his hand across the blanket and rested it on top of hers before he slid closer and wrapped his arm around her shoulders.

"This Puck guy is crazy," he whispered in her ear, and she shivered, leaning into his strong frame.

The rest of the play was a blur. Her senses were consumed by Tannis's touch – his strong arm around her shoulder, the lean length of his leg against hers, the brush of his fingertips right at the swell of her breasts.

How could she focus on anything else with his nearness a complete distraction? And if he could kiss like that . . . What else might his lips do, and where?

Then the play was over, Puck had not offended, and the afternoon had truly passed as though a dream. Long purple shadows fell across the park as they walked back to his car, yet the air was still hot.

Tannis tossed the picnic basket into the back seat and walked Sabrina to the passenger side. He made to lift the handle, then slammed the door shut and pressed her against the heated metal of the car. Her eyes widened in surprise.

And in expectation.

Her heart thudded in her chest as his lush eyes raked over her, consuming her, mesmerizing her just as his lips had done before. Tannis shifted so his hips and thighs crushed against hers. He lifted his thumb to her lower lip, rubbing it as his tongue had with their first kiss, and those bright blue eyes flashed, darkening, an undeniable magnetism crackling between them, drawing them closer.

Sabrina lifted her chin a bare centimeter, giving him permission to do more, to take more. His thumb snaked over her bottom lip to her top lip, then over her cheek until his palm cupped her jaw.

"Do you want me?" he asked in a ragged whisper.

Oh God, did she want him. She'd never encountered someone so easygoing and so sexy at the same time. Tannis was every contradiction, everything she should deny, yet that made her desire him more. And that he wanted her was evident. His dick, encased behind his jeans, throbbed against her hip.

"Yes," she answered with urgency.

His hand moved from her jaw to the back of her neck and he threaded his fingers into her damp, slick hair at the base of her skull.

With an excruciatingly languid move, he shifted his chiseled face closer to hers. Sabrina held her breath, waiting, waiting for that moment when those sultry, masterful lips would claim hers. It happened so fast between one second to the next that she didn't know what was happening. First there was breath, and then his lips.

She wrapped her arms around his sun-warm shoulders and melted into him.

The soft pressure of his lips coaxed a sigh from her, as though he had all day to spend on her lips, learning every curve of her lips, the texture of her tongue, the taste of her mouth. No pressure, no hurry, no rushing to another body part. He was enjoying this moment on her lips. His focus, his desire, was her lips and lips alone.

Where the fuck did this guy learn to kiss?

When he lifted his head, he flipped his tawny hair and his hooded eyes studied her, asking the question his mouth didn't.

And she couldn't answer quick enough.

"My place. My roommate's gone."

Tannis drove back to her apartment. More like careened, his right hand on her bare thigh, her hand on his arm. Her fingertips tickling over his skin sent chills down his spine and made focusing on the road even harder.

Harder.

Christ, he was rock hard for her.

He parked and ran to her side of the car to open her door, but she was already out, her muscled legs deeply tanned against her white shorts, the shape of her tits outlined by her shirt that clung like an invitation. Her black lined eyes were half-open, sultry and fevered, and he wanted to get her inside, into her bed, or her couch, or the fucking floor. He didn't care.

Without stopping, he raced to her, cupping both sides of her jaw with his hands, and bent to kiss her, a wild, hotter-than-the-sun kiss, a licking, biting, tongue thrusting kiss that lingered right there in the parking lot.

Tannis swiveled her around and walked her backwards to her apartment door, his lips planted on hers. They didn't separate as they walked, and Sabrina only tugged away to unlock her door. Then her succulent lips were back, clinging to his mouth, opening for more.

He kicked the door closed and thrust her against the wall. Patience be dammed. Tannis craved her, wanted her, right now.

He lifted his head slightly, his eyes focused on her black gaze. Their chests met with each heavy, panting breath, and they shared their air, breathing in and out for each other.

Keeping one hand on the back of her neck, he drove her hard against the wall with the weight of his chest. His other hand dropped to her breast, circling and cupping it through her shirt. Her tit was full, plump in his hand. He pulled his lips away, until just their breath touched. Her eyes captivated him as they stared at each other. Then, her hand dropped to her shirt and she lifted the hem over her bra, giving him more access. Tannis panted harder as he traced the outline of her nipple through her lace bra.

Then his finger dropped lower, measured, slowly, trailing down her supple belly to the button of her shorts. His finger dipped beneath, then stopped.

They breathed together, their lips close enough to kiss but not kissing, and he waited. His heart pounded in his temples, but he wouldn't move that finger until she gave him permission. He might have her trapped against the wall, but he was Sabrina's to control. He was at her mercy, even if she didn't know it.

"Yes," she said again, her breath a kiss from a rose petal, and he ground against her, pinning her with even more force, but kept his hips shifted away so his hand had room to move.

With a flip of his finger and thumb, her button came undone and the zipper slid down with the girth of his hand. Then his fingertip was at the edge of her lacy panties, date panties, panties that said yes for her, but he would have her say it again. So again, he paused with that excruciating patience.

"Yes," she shivered as she whispered.

"Yes," he echoed in a sensual drawl and his finger moved, his calloused fingertip on the tender skin under her panties, slipping to her slit that was already wet. Her gasp was the only sound breaking the blood-pounding silence.

His finger slicked against her wetness, going deep down her slit to her opening, wetting his finger more, then slipping back up to her love button, her passion point. Sabrina dug her nails into his back, clutching to him as his finger swept over it once, again, then around, and Sabrina inhaled a high-pitched squeal.

His cock was hard, throbbing painfully against his jeans, begging, no demanding for release. He had to have her soon. But to see her sinfully black eyes glazed and sparkling, her skin shining under the effect of her climax, he also wanted to drag every moment with her out as long as he could. His finger remained between her legs, dripping with her sexy juices, and if he didn't move soon, he'd come in his pants.

Tannis rested his forehead on hers, and his gaze remained fixed on Sabrina's eyes.

Her shuddering began as waves, quivering waves created by his skillful finger, the tip of one digit that made her knees shake and her brain leave her body. Then his light touch became a ferocious dragging across her clit. Every cell in her body shattered as the quaking overwhelmed her, driving any and every thought from her head. She lowered her lids.

"No, look at me," Tannis commanded in a low growl, and her glassy eyes shifted to peer into his.

She clenched her thighs on his hand at her climax. Her jaw set as she groaned and shuddered in his arms, and then she went limp, with only his strong hand in her pants and the one at the back of her neck keeping her upright. His lips brushed against hers so lightly she wasn't even sure he kissed her.

Sabrina's breathing calmed, but her mind was still a dervish, uncontrolled. As she inhaled to catch her breath, his lips crushed hers, grinding into her teeth. His zipper sounded in the echoes of their breaths, and he worked them off his legs before thrusting his head backward. His face was hot, burning, making his tanned skin glow.

Flipping his shirt over his head and completely naked, he then pressed himself back into Sabrina, wrapping both arms around her waist. She slithered from the wall, dragging a fingernail across Tannis's tight, muscled abs – *oh, he was a vision of perfection!* – at once warm and smooth. In a fluid move of his powerful arms, he set her on the carpet.

Her shorts where already undone, and she wiggled them off her legs and whipped her shirt over her head. Her ponytail swung and swept over the sensitive nerves of her back. Every nerve she had was frenzied. Tannis's light eyes burned with a blue fire as he stood above her, watching her strip.

Sabrina's own stormy eyes raked over his sinewy muscles, his chiseled curves, and she followed those curves with her finger. His powerful tanned shoulder and chest muscles were carved by heaven itself. Playing ball had toned him to the point where he looked like he'd stepped from a Calvin Klein underwear ad. She tried to stop the thought before it formed, but it still slipped in. *What's he doing with her?* He shuddered as her fingers traced the lines of him.

Her gaze drifted from his impossibly handsome face to the defined ridges of his chest and abs, and lower to the jutting hip dimples. Below that, his dick thrust out in front of him and quivered in expectation. He was more than full sized, that she'd felt from his jeans, and just as tanned as the rest of him, but her eyes widened at his thickness, round and smooth and searching for her.

Sabrina reached her hand out to grasp it, feel that smoothness, then followed his lead. Her hand paused right before she touched him. The side of her mouth curled up in a taunting smile. And she waited.

Tannis's chest and cock quivered.

"Yes," he said in a hoarse voice, and her hand wrapped around his dick.

Her fingers didn't reach her thumb. His groan rose from deep inside his chest, lower from his belly, and her taunting smile became an empowered grin. He fell to his knees in front of her.

Tannis snaked his hand around her back to her bra, and with a deft flip of his fingers, her bra came undone and fell from her rounded breasts. Tannis cupped one tit in his hand, as though he was admiring it, rubbing his thumb across the nipple again and again. Lowering his head, he flicked his tongue over the nub, replacing his thumb, and drew another smothered moan from her lips.

He knew every touch, every place to lick or caress, like she was his instrument, and his hands created the music inside her, drawing it forth as sonorous moans from her lips.

All this from throwing a ball? The power in his hands, in his fingers, commanded her and drove her to ecstasy.

And she hadn't even had sex with him yet.

He'd driven her to unheard of heights with his lips, his tongue, his fingers.

If he was a master with his dick as well . . .

Suddenly he was hurried, and while her hands moved over his skin, touching his lightly haired chest, teasing his abs, he looped his fingertips into her panties, dragging the lace down her legs and tossing them across the room to land somewhere with her bra.

He was quick reaching for his discarded jeans, grabbing a condom out of the pocket and rolling it on in a heartbeat. Then he was leaning over her, his scent of musk blending with the heat of the day and the lingering remnants of his spicy cologne filling her senses. It was his scent, so remarkably Tannis, which made her head spin more.

Her hand seized his shoulders, and the heat emanating from his body threatened to burn her alive.

And she wanted that burning.

She'd burn to ash if he demanded it of her.

The tip of his cock was at her opening, and she clung to him, waiting. And he stopped.

His hands sunk into the carpet on either side of her, and only his hips touched hers, teasing her.

Yet, he didn't move, didn't press forward, and her pussy quivered, waiting.

His eyes, that fiery gaze that hadn't looked away since they exited the fucking car, bore into her. If his dick didn't touch her core, by God, that gaze did.

She breathed him in, her nails digging into his skin, marking him.

Still, he remained poised, clenched, unmoving.

His eyes narrowed. He wanted something from her.

Sabrina's eyes narrowed back. She knew what he wanted. How long would he wait there, quickening in expectation?

She didn't want to find out.

"Yes," she whispered into his ear and licked, the salty taste of his skin thick on her tongue.

Before she finished the word, he drove in deep, one swift thrust that rocked her to her core.

And she thought his *look* touched her core?

It was nothing compared to what the thickness of his dick did to her.

Once he was in, though, he seemed to lose that unconscionable control. He rode her fiercely, slapping his hips against hers fast, hard enough to redden her skin, and she wouldn't be able to walk normally for days. He stretched her beyond measure and when she thought she couldn't take anymore, he shifted so part of him rubbed against her lower lips, catching her clit as he thrust, and the inner and outer sensation twisted into an electric wave in Sabrina, unlike anything, *anything* she'd ever experienced, and she wasn't sure what she screamed in her climax.

She was certain Tannis smiled before he shifted again, pounding into her. His eyes may have been open, but hers slammed shut as she crested. His growling and groaning were the only things she registered before he shuddered, stiffening over her, then his chiseled body went limp, and his sweaty forehead rested against hers.

Sabrina tried to grab her thoughts, but they slipped through her fingers like water.

What had just happened? She'd heard of a meeting of the minds, a meeting of bodies, of a connection that changed people's lives. *Soul mates,* some said.

Is that what this was?

Because she'd never had a connection like this in her life.

It was so powerful, she shivered. Not from the sensation of Tannis pulling his dick from her, but from the sheer potency of what their bodies shared.

Maybe she had been wrong. Maybe it was too much, too soon. Maybe she was risking more than she realized.

Tannis rolled to her side onto the flat apartment carpet, hoping to cool the sweat that dripped between them and pooled on their skin. He wasn't just sweaty; he was sopping wet.

Sabrina had worked him hard, harder than he'd ever worked in a practice, in a game, anywhere.

And while his body was done, *done*, just the thought of fucking her again made his dick twitch.

He turned to her panting body and trailed his fingertips over her damp skin as she caught her breath. Over her snubbed nose and her full lips, across her neck to her tits and her dusky tan nipples, then over the subtle curve of her belly and hips, then back up again. Her skin popped into goose bumps, and she shivered.

"Oh, my," she breathed.

My sentiments exactly, Tannis thought. He didn't trust himself to speak yet.

She had commanded his body, his mind, his dick, so thoroughly, he was afraid of what he might say while his brain was still trying to rejoin his body.

Then he rolled onto his back and held her hand in his. They lay there on the floor for a long while, staring at the ceiling and waiting for their senses to return.

But in this quiet moment in the sunset light with the sounds of their breathing filling the room, he didn't want them to return anytime soon.

Her breasts rose high as she took a deep breath, then rolled to face Tannis. She propped her head on her hand, and Tannis did the same, and they resumed gazing into each other's eyes.

"What are we doing, Tannis?" she asked, uncertain if she truly wanted to hear his answer. Diana's words about his previous questionable fidelity and the ire of his friends rang in her head, and she wanted to put a stop to that ringing.

If all she got from him was this amazing day at the park followed by a night of mind-blowing sex (so cliche, but so true), then she'd accept it. She couldn't say she didn't know going in who he was, at least from the rumors.

But deep in her heart, she hoped it was more. Oh, God save her, she longed for it to be more. More of his easy smiles, more of his expressive sky-blue eyes, more of his magic fingers and dick. More of Tannis.

"What do you mean?"

At least he had enough grace to lift an eyebrow like he didn't know what she was asking. Her lips pressed together as she tried to form the words she didn't want to ask. Especially not right after what he put her body through.

"I know this is the worst time to ask, but I have to know. Is this all I get? Do we go back to tutor and student after this?"

Tannis sprung up on his extended arm and, with his tawny hair a mess, he reminded her of that nature show with

the little animals that popped up from the ground. Meerkats?
Focus, Sabrina!

"What do you mean?"

She bit her lip. "You have to know there are rumors about you, Tannis." Her voice was a wistful whisper, as though she didn't want the rumors to be true. And she didn't.

"So, you want to know if this is a date. And if you get to go to date number three? Like a game show?"

Ugh, it sounds so bad when he says it.

"No, not like that at all. But you have to know rumors say you only do a date or two, and then you move on. I just want to know if I should get my hopes up or not."

That smile, that lovely, easy smile shattered, and Tannis lowered himself onto Sabrina, covering her like a blanket.

"I'm not the athletic or cheerleader or partying type," she continued. "You might be missing the mark here."

She hated the words, hated the bare honesty that ripped from her chest. Tannis took her arms and extended them over her head, forcing Sabrina to look up at him, open and exposed, and tears burned in her eyes. She liked him too much. She'd lied when she talked to Diana. Sabrina had fallen for him on that first date, and now her heart was laid bare for a guy who was rumored to go through women like toilet paper.

"Do you know how beautiful you are?" he asked suddenly, and her heart stopped beating in her chest. He traced her face with his finger – her forehead, her nose, her jawline. "Your eyes are like dark pools I want to dive into, lose myself in. Your hair, I've never touched anything so soft in my life.

Your body? It's like you were made for me. Your skin is perfect, and your body fits mine like a glove."

"You would know." Sabrina tried to keep her voice steady as he kissed her shoulder.

"I used to do that, get around, a lot," he said as he nibbled at the curve of her neck. Then he lifted his head. "But lately, I haven't even done that. I'd go out, but not date. At first, I thought I was too young, too immature to be honest. And I just haven't found anyone I really wanted to date, someone who interested me, made me feel like it was worth it."

Sabrina didn't want to ask. She didn't. But his face was a breath from hers, holding her down just as much as his hand held her wrists. Though she wasn't sure her heart could handle the answer, she needed to know. Her blood hammered in her chest and temples.

"And now?"

His eyes were too intense, and *Oh God,* that sultry smile returned to his full, kissable lips.

"I think you're worth it."

Chapter Eight

THEY WERE STUPID giddy on campus once summer classes started. When they weren't in class or practice or tutoring, they were fucking and cuddling with each other, basking in the glow and heat they shared of just being Sabrina and Tannis, together. Sabrina hadn't thought a relationship with Tannis was possible, yet every day he did something to prove that he wanted to be with her. That he needed to be with her.

They each had one class, and Tannis came into the writing center once a week for his tutoring. At first, Sabrina was worried he wouldn't take it seriously, but he was all business when he attended their tutoring sessions. He only snuck a kiss when he first arrived. And when he left. And every chance he could find in between.

Several guys from his team noticed his behavior, his time with Sabrina – how could they not? Tannis was busy at summer training, working to stay in top shape during his off season and getting ready for fall ball. Enrique sat on an inclined bench near him, curling forty-five-pound dumbbells and asking Tannis about Sabrina. In a sudden rush, he dropped the dumbbells with a clang and stood over Tannis lifting on the flat bench.

"Just be careful. Some people are not as accepting as others."

"It's not like I'm dating a transformer or a plastic doll. She's a person. A college student just like us, and a damn good one at that. What the hell kind of comment is that anyway, Enrique?"

"Dude. I'm on your side. I don't give a rat's ass who you date as long as you're happy. But you know there are people who don't like new blood in their little group. Or they see anyone who's a little bit different as something bad or less than them."

"Sabrina's different because she's not a jock? Isn't in your clique? That's so high school and doesn't make any sense. We are freaking adults. Plus, she rooms with Diana, who *is* a volley baller."

"Yeah, but that doesn't make them friends, or mean they run in the same circles."

"Fuck off, Enrique."

"Dude, don't get pissed at me. I'm a friend and hell, I like her. She's cute and funny. Smart is sexy. And she's making sure your grades are high enough to stay on the team. That alone makes me her fan. But I've heard things, about trying to get you away from her. . ."

Tannis dropped the weighted bar into its frame. He turned his hard features to Enrique.

"What the fuck, Enrique? Who? Who the fuck cares who I date? This is the dumbest thing I've ever heard!"

Enrique's eyes lowered, finding his feet interesting as Tannis's voice overwhelmed everyone in the weight room who paused their lifting to stare in Tannis's direction. Tannis glared around the weight room, silently telling them to mind their own business.

"Is it Ken? And Gabe?"

Enrique remained quiet, rubbing his jaw with one calloused hand. His silence was the answer.

Tannis plopped back onto the weight bench. "What do they have against me?"

"Well, Ken wants that first string pitching position. And you are seen as this big man on campus. All the girls, and a lot of guys, like you. Other guys want to be you. You could date anyone, and to see you with a short brainiac like Sabrina doesn't jive with their worldview."

Tannis studied Enrique for a long moment, his anger at Enrique's words clashing with his gratefulness that his teammate had the *cajones* to say something to him. At least some of his team members had his back. And he knew it took courage for Enrique to say something. Tannis shifted and settled himself under his barbell to resume his lifting. He glanced at Enrique standing next to him.

"Sorry for losing it on you. I appreciate your information, as much as I hate hearing it. So, thanks for that, bro."

Enrique nodded and swiveled to return to his own dumbbell curls.

"And Enrique?" Tannis called out, his hands resting on the bar. Enrique looked over his shoulder.

"If they say anything else to you, tell them to get their chicken shit asses over to talk to me. I'll set them straight."

There was no ambiguity in Tannis's words. Though he had an easy disposition, his pitching arm was a pummeling device when he reached his boiling point. Enrique would make it known that Tannis was getting close to that point.

Tannis's mind flicked back crazily to his Shakespeare conversation with Sabrina, when she dared him to name a play other than Romeo and Juliet. Forget Puck and his crew – right now he felt like he was *living* through a version of Romeo and Juliet. In this day and age? How had that one hit so close to home? He shook his head. Focusing on his barbell, Tannis strained to lift the weight and took out his aggressions in sweat.

Sabrina was one of the three summer tutors, and she worked as much as she could. Especially since she was fronting the entire apartment by herself for the next two and a half months.

The privacy, however, was well worth it. She hoped Diana wouldn't mind the noise once she came back for the fall semester – if Sabrina was still with Tannis, that was. And with how amazing everything was going, she had no reason to believe otherwise. It was like a dream.

Tannis came to his afternoon tutoring session on Wednesday. The week had been busy for them both – between the condensed school semester, her work, and his training, they hadn't seen each other since the weekend. A few texts, nothing more.

But when he collapsed into the chair across from her with a tattered stack of papers in his hand (some things never change – every homework assignment, essay, project, was a collection of stained and ratty papers), his easy smile didn't materialize quite as easily.

"Everything Ok?" she asked as she pulled his papers to her side of the table.

His smile widened immediately, calming his tanned face and popping his dimples. Maybe she'd imagined his discomfort?

"Yeah. Summer training is going good. And I think, if I can keep up with this class, I might pull a B. Shocker. Right?"

He's so cute, she thought before speaking. "Not quite a shocker, but it would be a great accomplishment. Let's see what we can do to get you that B."

Lifting a pen, Sabrina flicked a wary gaze at Tannis. "You sure nothing's bugging you?"

Tannis sprung up from his chair and, whipping his head from side to side to make sure no one was looking, he landed a quick kiss on her surprised lips.

"Positive. Just focused on this class."

She walked him through the paper, going over grammar mistakes and giving advice on areas of development.

When they were done, a few minutes remained before he had to head out for summer training at the fields.

"Damon's having a get together this weekend. Saturday night. You wanna go?"

With so many students gone for the summer, parties had been scarce. Tannis hadn't mentioned any since the one she took Diana to, and Damon was throwing another one. Diana wouldn't be there as her wing woman, but this time Sabrina knew more people. And Tannis would be there.

Now's not the time to stop risk-taking!

"Yeah. It would be nice to get out and do something after this week."

"You mean do something other than spend more time with me between your legs."

"Tannis!" she squealed, her cheeks burning. What if someone heard him?

"No, it's all good. I haven't been to a party in weeks."

"A party, not a get-together?" Sabrina asked, and this time Tannis's cheeks brightened in a rosy glow, and it made his dusky skin even more stunning.

Not for the first time, she wondered what he was doing with her. He called her beautiful, said she was amazing, but how did that measure up to someone like him, a veritable Greek god on campus?

"Same difference with Damon. You up for it? No big exams to study for? No papers?"

One sleek black eyebrow rose on Sabrina's forehead. "Will that drunk John guy be there?" she asked.

Tannis shook his head. "Ho, no. He has been uninvited from Damon's parties. So, no homework?" he pressed.

She shrugged. "Even if I did, I'd still have Sunday to catch up. Yeah, it'd be fun."

Tannis stood and came around to her side of the table. Bending low, he placed one of his delicate kisses on her ready lips.

"Ok, I'll try to swing by after training on Friday, but if I don't see you, I'll be at your place around six on Saturday? That Ok?"

"Yeah," she breathed. He grinned at her, then turned and walked out of the writing center. She rested her face on her hand and watched the view of his tight ass until the door closed behind him. Then she sighed and started her tutoring write up as she waited for her next student.

Her phone lit up as she was leaving the building. Sabrina juggled her bag to dig out her phone. Diana's self-possessed pic lit up her screen.

"Hey Di! How are you? How's your summer going?"

"Ugh, so much work. I'm working over forty hours a week but socking that money away to pay for our apartment and books. I'm so grateful for my volleyball scholarship, but I just wish it covered a bit more."

"I get that," Sabrina agreed.

She was fortunate that her academic scholarship covered her books and classes, and gave her a small, very small stipend for her apartment. And it assigned her the job at the writing center. Poor Diana always stressed about money and because of her volleyball schedule, she couldn't work much. Saving up her summer money kept Diana flush for the year.

"How are things going with Tannis? I haven't spoken to you in a week!"

"I texted you about it after our date last weekend," Sabrina countered.

"Huh," Diana huffed in her ear. "*It was fun*? That doesn't tell me anything! I want all the juicy details."

Sabrina laughed into the phone.

"What?" Diana asked. "I don't have a boyfriend right now. I have to live vicariously through you until fall when I can have a social life again."

"Ok, ok. No, we are doing well together. I almost can't believe it."

"Have you slept with him yet? God, I hope so. And I hope his dick is as built as the rest of him."

"Diana!"

"What? I said vicariously!"

"Still . . ." Sabrina wracked her brain to find a new topic.

"You deserve someone like him. Not only is he hot, he's a nice guy. Not what you'd expect, right? So, have you? Slept with him?"

Sabrina rolled her eyes to the darkening sky. She hesitated to admit she'd slept with him right after their second date. Diana would love that.

"Well, if you hadn't left for the summer, you would have heard us and not had to ask me that question."

There, subtle implication. Diana was a smart girl. She'd get it.

And she did.

"A-ha! And is it?"

Sabrina rounded into the main campus parking lot.

"Is what *what*?"

"Does his package match the wrapper?" Diana asked coyly.

Sabrina licked her lips.

"Better than the wrapper," she answered, her cheeks flaming hot again, and not from the scorchingly hot summer air.

"I knew it!" Diana cheered.

Sabrina lifted her keys as she approached her car, and when she got to her parking space, she froze.

"Sabrina, are you there? Did I lose you?"

"What the hell – "

"Sabrina!" Diana yelled in a high-pitched panic. "Are you Ok?"

Sabrina blinked back a well of burning tears.

"No, Diana. No, I'm not."

Her car. Well, her tires. What had been a perfectly running car, if a bit of a gas guzzler, that morning now sat on two, no *three* flat tires.

How did I get three flats?

Blinking didn't work. Tears ran over her cheeks. How was she going to afford to fix this?

"Sabrina!"

"My car," Sabrina whispered in a weepy voice as she circled her car in disbelief.

"What's wrong with your car?"

"I have a flat, Diana," Sabrina sobbed. "Three flats."

Diana waited two heartbeats before responding.

"Three flat tires." It wasn't a question.

"Yeah," Sabrina cried. She stood at the back of her car. What did she do now? Call a tow? How much did that cost?

"Three," Diana intoned. Her voice caught Sabrina's attention.

"Yeah. Three, why?"

"Motherfuckers." Diana was pissed. Her voice was a knife, cutting through the phone.

"What? Who motherfuckers?"

Sabrina could hear Diana breathing heavily through the phone.

"Brin? Are you in a safe location? Can you give me five minutes to help you fix this?"

"What? Why —"

"Don't do anything for five minutes. I'll call you back. Don't call anyone. No one. Not even Tannis. Give me five. Promise?"

"Tannis is still in training I think." Her brain wasn't functioning. That didn't answer Diana's question at all.

"Promise me. No one."

"Yeah. Yeah."

"Ok," Diana's tone shifted, becoming more caring, almost motherly. "Get in your car and wait."

Sabrina did as Diana directed, thankful someone seemed to know what to do because Sabrina sure as hell didn't. How much did one tire cost? Three tires? She punched in a local tire place and her chest dropped to her feet. *Over a hundred dollars per tire? For the cheap ones? And how much for labor?*

Her phone buzzed in her hand, and Sabrina punched the answer button.

"Ok, I just spoke to my parents," Diana said in a rush, "and we are going to send you some money on your money app, about fifty bucks. You need to scrape together another fifty. Can you get that or call your parents?"

Sabrina wiped at her tear-stained cheeks. "I got fifty in savings." What was Diana doing?

"Ok, I called Damon. He's a car guy and I thought he'd have a solution. He's got a friend with a tow and they are going to tow your car to that friend's shop. You can't get new tires for a hundred, but Damon can put recycled tires on your car and get you going for that amount."

Fresh tears poured down Sabrina's cheeks. What an incredibly loyal friend she had in Diana. "And you are giving me fifty for it? Why?"

"Sweetie. Friends help each other out. And you saved my ass with this summer situation, so I'll do everything I can to

103

help you. I know you don't think of yourself this way, but you are one of my best friends, and I'll have your back every time. Now, Damon is on his way with his friend and the truck. Damon will drive you by the bank. Give him the money, and he will take you to his friend's shop and you should be on your way in a few hours."

Sabrina nodded into the phone. Her thoughts were slowing weaving back together.

"Why didn't you want me to call Tannis?" It had seemed like a strange request.

Diana sighed into the phone.

"I spoke to Chelle earlier in the week. She mentioned he'd been getting pretty serious shit from several guys on the team, and he doesn't need to think that he's responsible for this or anything. Some people are just shit heads, Brin, and if we can minimize that, keep that shit from staining too many people, then we should. He doesn't need the stain of this on top of all that."

Sabrina nodded to herself. "You're right. You're right. And I'll get you that fifty back as soon as I can."

"Nope," Diana told her. "Consider it a gift. Love you, girl. Wait for Damon."

Damon pulled up in a sporty, tri-colored sedan and leapt out to direct the tow truck driver to Sabrina's sad-looking car. He'd thrown a black button-down over his white tank top but didn't button it and the hem flapped in the breeze.

"Hey, Sabrina. What the hell happened here?" He crouched to the ground and poked a finger at the tires. "Yeah, someone slashed them. Who the hell did you piss off? Tell a student to write the wrong word in a paper?"

Through her tears, a bubble of laughter escaped at Damon's attempt to lighten the situation. She wiped her face with her sleeve again.

"I don't know what happened. Diana said something about guys bugging Tannis?"

Damon swatted his hand in the air. "Ignore all that. Some people never left high school." Then Damon stood and helped the other man get the car on the tow bed. The words "Medina Tow" were emblazoned on the cab and the sides of the bed.

After the car was set, the other man came over to Damon and Sabrina.

"Hey, man." He gave Damon a fist bump and turned to Sabrina. "Hey, I'm Carlo Medina. Damon said a friend got in a fix and we needed to help. Three tires, that's a shitty thing to do."

"Thanks Carlo. I appreciate it. And yeah, it's expensive."

Carlo shook his head. His slick black hair hadn't moved the entire time he worked.

"Naw. It's more than that. Like, insurance? If you have decent comprehensive, they'll cover four flat tires. Usually with no out of pocket. That's why it's shit to do three tires. Insurance don't cover that."

"Yeah," Damon added. "My boy Carlo here, he usually sees guys in nice cars in for this. Crazy ex's will slice three tires."

Sabrina gripped the handle of her bag, her eyes wide. "What? That's a thing?"

Carlo tugged his thick work gloves off his hands. "Yeah, it's a thing. You good, Damon? See you in a bit?"

"Yeah. Let me get Sabrina to the bank and we'll meet you there. Thanks, brother."

"No problem. See you at the shop. Nice to meet you, Sabrina," Carlo called out with a wave. He swung the door of the truck cab wide and jumped up to the driver's seat.

Damon held out his arm to his car. "Your carriage awaits. Let's get you back up and running, Sabrina."

Once they were settled in the waiting area of the car shop and Sabrina had handed over her one hundred bucks (*thank God for Diana's extra cash!*), Damon and Sabrina sat in the hard plastic chairs to wait.

"Are you going to tell Tannis about this?" Damon asked.

Sabrina dropped her head into her hands, letting her sleek black hair form a curtain to shut out the world.

"Diana said not to call him tonight," she said from under her hair. "But she also said something about people he knows who don't like me. She didn't say it outright, but the suggestion was that they might have done this."

Damon rubbed the thin trace of a mustache on his lip, taking his time before answering.

"Yeah, I'd heard something about that."

"I mean, he's going to find out anyway. If his buddies don't brag about it, he could easily overhear someone else talking about it. If I knew my friends or my boyfriend was hiding something this big, I'd be pissed."

That silent, pensive pause again.

"Your boyfriend?"

Sabrina sat up hard and turned her gaze on Damon.

"Well, I mean, we've been dating for a couple of weeks. I just assumed. . ."

"Hey, you don't have to defend it to me. I'm rooting for you guys, and I think Tannis feels the same about you. This – " he shook his hand toward the noise coming from the shop, "this makes things more difficult. If you want my advice, wait until this is taken care of so he doesn't feel like he has to jump through hoops to rescue you. It's already going to be hard enough. But call him tonight. Tell him what happened. Let him know that your friends, and by that I mean people who are friends to both of you, had your back. Then move forward. A lot of people like to hold others back. Don't let that happened to you."

Damon patted her knee as he spoke. Sabrina wiped away more tears that threatened to fall. Damon was like a college yogi.

"Are you studying to be a Tibetan Monk? Because you're like a wise oracle or something."

A slight smile tugged at Damon's overly serious face. He had resting bad-ass face, and the smile cracked that hard veneer.

"Yeah. It's my major. Just so you know, Sabrina, I know you didn't expect to be friends with someone like me, but now that you are, I'll always have your back. My boy Carlo will be done soon. Get home, get settled, and then call Tannis. That's an order from your Tibetan Monk."

Chapter Nine

"WAIT, WHAT?"

Tannis didn't react well to the news about her car tires. But then, she hadn't expected him to.

"Don't be mad, babe. Diana helped me out. She called Damon, even sent me a bit of money, and Damon and his friend Carlo got me refurbished tires or something like that, and my car's as good as new!"

"Did you call the cops? Campus police?"

Sabrina sat at her tiny dining table that she used for everything but eating. That happened on the couch in front of the TV. Several textbooks and folders littered the table, and

Sabrina picked at one with a nervous finger. Her video call with Tannis was not a bright idea – watching his anger darken his bright face made her chest clench.

"No, I didn't think of it. And Damon didn't say anything about that."

Tannis let out a long huff, and his shining eyes narrowed even more. Other than the night at the party with the drunk John, she'd never seen him with anything other than an open, engaging face. This dark, hard expression, it wasn't Tannis.

"They couldn't have done much anyway. It's not like they have video out there. But I have an idea of who did it." His jaw twitched as he spoke.

"I just want to let it go. If you do know who did it, just ignore it. Any attention will just make everything worse. We got the car fixed and it's like it never happened. If we ignore it, we keep the upper hand. You know?"

Sabrina's hand moved to her hair, pulling it into a sleek ponytail over her shoulder as she spoke. Tannis's eyes softened over the video.

"Ok, babe. Are you Ok otherwise? Do you want me to come over?"

She did. She badly wanted him to come over. To hold her and tell her everything would be all right. To fall asleep in his arms. But that stack of books and folders demanded more of her time. She sighed.

"I do, but I have a stack of studying that I didn't get done earlier because I was in the car shop. How about we meet for lunch or something on campus tomorrow? Can you do that?"

"Even if I couldn't, I'd make it happen. Do you have to be up early for class? Or can you at least sleep in if you have to study late?"

Sabrina's stomach fluttered, and she twined her finger in her hair. If they weren't officially calling each other boyfriend and girlfriend, he at least sounded like a boyfriend. She smiled into the phone.

"Thank you for worrying about me. I get to sleep in a bit, but I'll meet you right at noon at the cafeteria?"

Tannis nodded. "Yeah. I can't wait."

"Ok, then, I'll see you tomorrow. Bye, babe."

"Love ya. Bye Sabrina."

Then he hung up, and the phone dangled from Sabrina's fingertips as she tried to regain her brain. *Love ya?*

Had they reached that point? So soon? Did he really love her?

And just as importantly, did she love him?

She flipped her hair over the back of her chair and looked up at the ceiling.

They were going to have to have a talk soon.

Not tomorrow. Maybe after the party this weekend.

But soon.

Sabrina looked fine at lunch the next day when Tannis met up with her, but maybe she was hiding her anger or frustration over the night before. Tannis had called Damon right after he'd hung up with Sabrina and thanked him. Then he had also asked if Damon knew anything about the tires. Damon had told him the same he'd told Sabrina and ended the phone call with a piece of sage advice that struck Tannis for several reasons.

"Your girl, Sabrina, she handled it well. If she says ignore it, try to ignore it. But I know you, Tannis. And if you feel you need to protect your girlfriend, then I got your back."

He hung up with Damon in a bit of shock. Damon had called Sabrina his girlfriend, and Tannis had said *love ya* when he hung up with Sabrina.

And that was the problem.

Even though he called her his girlfriend to anyone who would listen, they hadn't actually defined that part of their relationship yet.

And he'd said *love ya* before defining it, too. The emotion had just poured from him, a wave of truth. But what if she wasn't ready for that yet? What if he overstepped?

He rubbed his hands through his hair. *Fuck it.* He'd never tip-toed around anyone in his life, and he wasn't about to start with Sabrina. He'd rather she knew how much he cared for her and risk it than *not* let her know.

Everything in life was a risk. Pitching a curve ball was a risk. Bunting was a risk. Going to college was a risk. And when he saw Sabrina approaching him in the cafeteria, he knew he'd risk anything for her. No matter what anyone else said. Or did.

In a tacit agreement, they skimmed over Sabrina's tires, and neither said anything about Tannis's goodbye on the phone. They had less than an hour to eat and chat, and they kept it light.

The most important thing for Tannis was knowing that Sabrina was Ok. He promised to stop by on Friday after training and bring fast food for dinner.

And that phone call would have to be part of their conversation that night. He was sure of it.

Tannis's furious tunnel vision focused on Ken as he stormed into the field where Ken was warming up. Without a break in his stride, he marched up to Ken and shoved him into the chain link fence.

"What the hell, Reyes?"

"No, what the hell with *you*, Xiao?" Tannis pressed his arm into Xiao's neck. "Why are you messing with my girlfriend? Slashing her tires? You're lucky I didn't sick Damon and his cronies on you!"

"Are you fucking threatening me, Reyes?" Xiao twisted and thrust Tannis's arm away. "And I don't know what you're talking about."

Tannis's lips tightened. Ken had never been a good liar.

"You do know what I'm talking about. And if you didn't do it, then you know who did."

Ken's mouth curved up into a snide smile. "You were warned, Reyes. Your *girlfriend* is a geeky nobody and there's lots of people who aren't happy with her. Not just me. You can do better, brother. And you and I and everyone else know it."

Ken spat into the dirt. "And even if I did know who slashed her tires, I wouldn't tell you. Because I don't turn my back on my friends."

Tannis's eyes thinned into a hard glare. "What does that mean?"

"If you weren't at practice, we'd never see you. You're changing. You aren't here for your friends. You get this new girl and dump us. People aren't happy about that, either. You might want to think about that, Reyes."

Ken moved to brush past, but Tannis grabbed his shirt.

"You see, Xiao, that's where you're wrong. I didn't turn my back on anybody. My friends, my real friends, my real brothers and teammates, they're happy for me and welcoming to Sabrina. They aren't self-involved stuck-ups who treat people like shit." He thrust Ken away. "And you better tell whoever did slash her tires, that if I find out who did it, they're gonna regret it. Now get your two-faced ass outta my face."

Tannis gave him another shove, and Ken tripped over his own feet as he left.

"Reyes! Xiao! Do I need to come over there and tear you a new one?" Coach Alzugaray yelled.

Tannis's lip screwed up as he watched Ken walk away. "No, Coach. Here we come."

Tempting

When Sabrina walked into the empty apartment after work on Friday, she dropped her backpack on the table and flopped into the chair. She needed to study — she'd lost so much time having her car worked on – and between that and Tannis, she hadn't been able to focus on her heavy soc textbook. But even as she tugged her sociology text from her bag, she knew she still wouldn't be able to focus.

Books and papers were scattered across the tabletop. Right now, everything in front of her was a blur, and studying was the last thing on her mind.

Tannis had been casual at lunch, nothing uncomfortable or strained between them, as if saying *love ya* over the phone was the most natural thing in the world.

But if you loved someone, wasn't it?

Sabrina took out her pen, as though she were going to use it and ended up nibbling on the tip as her brain concentrated on Tannis.

Fixating on his bright, dancing eyes, that lazy smile that made her insides churn until she thought she'd lose her mind, his broad chest and the easy laugh that came from it regularly. The way he kissed her like they had all time in the world. The way he made her feel like there was no one else in the room whenever he turned that blue gaze on her.

Were his words honest? Did he love her?

And did she love him?

Those questions tossed over and over in her mind like a ship on the waves.

They were young. They'd both dated before, but this sensation, had she ever felt like this? Was it possible to find a serious relationship when everything else around them said don't take it seriously?

And a jock, a popular ball player — what was she thinking? Could someone like him fall for a girl like her?

Maybe in a campy romance movie, that is, she thought.

More than that, everything about Tannis was so nonchalant. Could he even be serious in a relationship? She'd not seen him be serious about much of anything. He was even lighthearted about his practices and games!

Sabrina shook her head.

Yet, maybe they weren't as different as they seemed. Maybe it was only because of the way she'd seen herself for the past few years. She bit harder on the end of her pen, leaving teeth marks in the plastic. Maybe Diana and Damon were right. She *was* more than just a brain. And maybe that's why she and Tannis worked so well together. They weren't opposites; they were compliments.

Love ya.

So many questions.

And no answers.

Do I love him?

The ceaseless line of questions kept her distracted as her eyes glazed over. A sudden knock at the door made her jump and she glanced at the clock.

Whoa. She'd spent an hour pondering those two words?

Tannis lifted a white take-out bag when she opened the door.

"Tacos? It's dollar Friday at Don Jose's."

He landed a peck on her cheek as he stepped through the door and set the bag on the edge of the chaotic table.

His eyes scanned the stacks of books and papers that covered the surface.

"Busy studying? I'm sorry that your tires threw a wrench in your works, if you were trying to get work done this week. I asked Ken about your car at practice, but he denied anything, of course."

Tannis may have glossed over that conversation with Ken, but she could imagine how that went – she almost felt badly for Ken. *Almost.* Tannis's tone was so apologetic, Sabrina melted inside. He gave her a slight smile, his dimples deep and inviting.

Is this love?

To notice these little things that made her heart soar? To have her heart flutter when he gazed at her with those intense cerulean eyes that perfectly matched his shirt? To find such joy when he did something as simple as pick up dinner or notice she was studying?

Yes. Yes, that's exactly what it was. She wasn't going to question it, bring it up, make him explain it. She didn't need any of that. If he said the L word, if she said it, who cared? Sabrina loved him. Tannis loved her. And she seemed to feel it more every time she looked at him. She wasn't going to bring

117

up her tires or how others judged their relationship or his glib words on the phone.

He was here. With her. Feeding her tacos and worrying about her grades.

That was all the proof she needed.

Sabrina laced her arms around his shoulders, and he turned into her embrace.

"What's this?" he asked as he nuzzled her neck, his voice muted. "Aren't you hungry?"

"Not for food," she whispered in a husky voice as she walked him into her bedroom.

The tacos were cold when they finally ate.

Chapter Ten

SABRINA SLID A last layer of bright red lipstick over her lips when the knock came at her door that Saturday night. She didn't usually do something as bold as red, but she was feeling bold. Tannis made her feel bold, and she wanted to show it off. She pursed her lips and made several kissing puckers with her lips as she walked to the living room.

She answered the door and Tannis's eyes went round as he looked her up and down.

"Whoa."

Her legs were darkly tanned from the summer sun and toned from walking, and her short skirt showed them off well.

119

She wore a shirt that was cut short and showed off a sliver of her midriff. Her dark hair and bright red lips made a statement, she knew. But to see their effect on Tannis sent a fiery flare through her, and she smiled widely.

She grabbed her purse from the couch and locked her door.

"Let's go."

Tannis's light blue t-shirt showcased his lean frame and broad shoulders. His tight jeans clung to his perfectly rounded ass and powerful legs. His tawny hair was brushed in soft waves to the side, and Sabrina could have spent the night doing nothing but watching him. *What party?*

A few people were at Damon's when they arrived, and Tannis poured red cups of Sprite for Sabrina and himself. "Unless you want something harder?" he asked.

He never judged, never assumed. It was easy to understand why his friends were worried about whom he dated. She merely wished they weren't taking it out on her. Or Tannis.

The last time she had attended a party at Damon's, that drunk guy had invaded her personal space, and since she didn't know what to expect for this night, she decided to keep it clean. Plus, she could enjoy the image Tannis presented more when she wasn't drinking.

She'd get drunk on Tannis.

They sat in the back around the fire pit with Damon and Romeo, and Tannis held her hand or put his arm around her shoulders as they sat and chatted. As if he wanted everyone to know they were dating. That they were, maybe, boyfriend and girlfriend?

As more people arrived later in the night, the house became cramped and the partiers grew more and more intoxicated, louder.

Gabe and Ken had arrived with a squadron of girls that Sabrina didn't recognize. She nudged Tannis when they came into the backyard, and he twisted around to look where she pointed.

"You know them?" she asked.

"No. They could be friends from Ken's hometown, or ball bunnies. You know, girls that are like groupies for ball players?"

Sabrina hugged her hand against her chest. "That's a thing?"

Tannis's shoulders shook as he chuckled. "Yeah. All sports have their group of women who want to bang a jock. And most have that *one* sport they go for. Baseball, soccer, football, basketball, you pick it, there's a group of women who want to date the players."

Sabrina studied the women with Gabe and Ken. Could one of them have slashed her tires? Could it have been Ken or Gabe? Would they do that to the girlfriend of one of their teammates? What if they didn't know Tannis and Sabrina were boyfriend and girlfriend? Maybe they thought it was Ok because she and Tannis weren't official yet?

Or would that have not made a difference? They did it *because* Tannis and Sabrina were dating? Tannis spoke to her, asked her a question, and she was so absorbed in her thoughts that she missed it.

"Pardon?"

121

"You Ok staying out here? Or you want to go inside?" His eyes flicked at Ken's group that was nearing the fire pit.

Sabrina settled into her chair with a smug expression on her face.

"It's nice out here. Romeo and Damon are good company. I'm fine if you are."

Tannis's eyes crinkled to slits, and he leaned in close to her ear.

"What a bold woman you are. Do you know how sexy this smug look is on you?"

A dull fire erupted between her legs and spread through her entire body, and she threaded her fingers through Tannis's as she seized his gaze, kissing him lightly with her eyes wide open.

Was she claiming her man in front of Ken's crowd? *Maybe.* Was it juvenile and silly? *Probably.* Did it feel wonderful to show the world that Tannis was her man? *Definitely.*

She glanced over at Damon who winked at her.

They turned back to the fire pit and resumed their joking when someone bumped into Sabrina's chair. She jostled forward and spilled her Sprite on her lap and Tannis's jeans.

"Oh, sorry – " she started.

Tannis spun to the person behind them.

"What the hell —?"

Ken and a blonde neither of them knew stood right against Sabrina's chair, with Gabe and a few other people behind him.

"Ken, are you drunk? Watch what you're doing," Tannis told him before turning his attention back to Sabrina's wet skirt.

"You need to watch what you're doing," Ken answered ominously.

Tannis's hand froze on Sabrina's leg.

"What the hell does that mean?" Tannis asked him as his easy smile slipped away into a stony glare.

"Why do you keep bringing her around? She's not like us. We have a set group, and you bring her around. You think dating her will help keep up your GPA and keep you on the team? If your dumb ass is using her for your grades, then at least let us know."

Sabrina's mouth fell open in a wide *O*. Was that true? Was he using her for tutoring, sex, or just whatever he could get? It couldn't be, not after their time together, not after the loving words he'd spoken to her or how he'd been nearly attached to her side over the past few weeks.

Could it?

Had she misread this relationship that much? She hadn't heard him call her his girlfriend yet, even if he did say he loved her. Or rather, *love ya*.

Is he using me?

Tannis rose and pushed past his lawn chair, knocking it on its side. His face had completely transformed. Gone was the lighthearted, Southern California handsome ball player. In his place was a hard and angry man, his face darkening as the shadows of the fire flicked across him. His jaw set in a firm line, and his fists clenched hard enough to turn his knuckles white.

Another set of screeching sounds, and Damon and Romeo stood up behind him.

Ken puffed out his chest to the slightly taller Tannis, trying to make himself seem larger, a trick he'd tried to pull off since they both started on the Hawks baseball team. As he stood before Ken, the bright red rage that boiled under Tannis's skin blinded him to everything else but this man who just insulted his girlfriend, the woman he loved, and his relationship with her.

The skittering sound of patio chairs against the cement permeated the rage in his head, and he knew that Damon and Romeo were standing behind him in solidarity. Tannis flexed his biceps, ready to pound Ken into the ground.

"Why don't you just tell her you're using her?" Ken taunted, his own ruffled, dark hair making glinting in the firelight and making him seem like a devil to Tannis.

Tannis's arm flew before he registered its movement, connecting with Ken's jaw in a solid hit. Ken's face snapped back, and he stumbled backwards with the force of the blow.

"Who the fuck do you think you are, Ken. Talking like that?"

Ken's words were intended to hurt, to wound Sabrina in the worst way, and Tannis would make him pay for putting those doubting thoughts in Sabrina's head. Tannis pressed forward to Ken, flexing his fingers, readying his right hand for another hit. Ken launched forward, thrusting his shoulder into Tannis's belly and slamming him into the now-abandoned patio chairs. Tannis's arm struck the metal of the fire pit and knocked it to the side. Tannis's arm scorched, inflaming red and blistering where his skin tapped the edge.

Ken tried to get Tannis on the ground, but Tannis was faster, rolling onto his knees and Ken onto his back. Tannis had the upper hand, burnt arm or no, and pummeled his ferocious pitcher's fist into Ken's face again.

Tannis saw nothing, felt nothing — not his friends yelling, not Sabrina's shocked face, not the footsteps of those running around the patio. It faded to black. His focus tunneled solely on Ken's bruised face. His entire body burned with fury, and he was willing to do anything, anything, to make Ken pay for what he said about Sabrina. For how he had treated her the past few weeks.

He pulled his arm back, preparing to land another solid hit on Ken's nose, when a hand grabbed his wrist, stopping him.

Tannis whirled around to find Damon's black gaze boring into him and Damon's giant hand on his wrist.

"Let me go, Damon."

Tannis wasn't done with Ken. He'd beat this fucker to a pulp and teach him a lesson. But he wasn't done with Ken alone. His eyes scanned the fearful faces of Ken's friends.

"Which one of you assholes slashed Sabrina's tires?"

No one answered, but everyone's eyes suddenly found the ground more interesting than the fight. Tannis lunged, but Damon's vice-like grip held tight.

"No. Reyes, Ken knows he fucked up. He's done. You can lose your scholarship if you keep going. Don't be like me. Keep your ass in school, keep your girl. And like it or not, he's your teammate. We'll get this fucker and his friends out of the house for you. Don't touch him again, or you'll really have trouble."

Damon's soothing tone permeated the dark fog that surrounded Tannis in his anger. Tannis's bulging arm unclenched, his muscles relaxing, and some of the fury wracking his body alleviated. With Damon's hand still on his wrist, Tannis stepped off Ken and back to Sabrina. She had fled the fire pit area and stood near the house, watching the disturbing events unfold. A tight expression of horror was plastered across her delicate features and crushed Tannis's heart.

He reached out a hand, and a spike of hot alarm flared in his chest when she recoiled from it.

"He's lying, Sabrina. Please, you have to know he was lying, making something up. You know how I feel about you. What we have, you can't fake that. I know I can't. Please, Sabrina."

He was begging. Pleading. Desperate. But he would get on his knees to beg if that's what it took to get her to stay.

"Please, Sabrina. You know how I feel. What we feel. Please."

Sweat dripped from his hair down his neck. Between the warm temperature, his fight with Ken, the pure fire of rage and desperation that burned inside him, the neckline of his shirt was wet.

"Why would he say that, Tannis?" she asked in a quiet voice. He didn't blame her for her hesitation, but he did hate it. "Are you using me to get better grades? For sex? For the hell of it?"

He shook his head. "No, not at all. Everything I've said to you, everything I've been with you, I've been open and honest. Think Sabrina. Think of everything you've been told by others, about some of the shit my so-called friends and teammates have been saying about you, about us. What's the easiest way to get rid of you if they didn't like you?"

Sabrina's deep black eyes were watery in the dying embers of the flickering firelight. Her lips pursed hard as she considered Tannis's words.

"What I told you last night," he continued, "that was the truth. I was laying my heart bare for you, and I'm doing it again now."

He risked stepping closer, narrowing the chasm of distance that separated them. He needed to touch her, to make that connection to her. When she didn't back up but let him come to her, that rock of agony in his belly lightened.

Then he extended his hand and took her hand in his. He exhaled a shaky breath when she didn't pull away.

"I love you, Sabrina, in a crazy, unexpected way that I didn't know was possible. I would never, never use you like that. I just want you to be happy, for us to be happy." He stepped closer and took her other hand. "I just want to be happy with you."

She lifted her face to his, her eyes shining in the dark. Her skin was smooth, dewy from the heat of the day and her reaction to seeing him fight, and he leaned into her and kissed her forehead, tasting the toasted salt of her and relishing the heat she gave off.

"And this fight? I've never seen you have a temper like that, Tannis. What is this?"

He wrapped his arms around her, and instead of stiffening, which was what he expected, she placed her arms around his waist.

"No. It takes a lot to set me off. But when it comes to you, Sabrina, I have no filter. I have no control. And if I think you're in danger or someone might hurt you, I won't hold back at all. I'll strike first and ask questions second. Because there is nothing more important to me in the world than you."

His words took her breath away, so when he grabbed her face and kissed her, she had nothing left. Everything she had was consumed by Tannis, then he and his kiss demanded more. And for this man who lifted her higher than anything else in his life? She would willingly give him everything she had. Sabrina gasped for breath and kissed him back, their lips attacking each other as if they couldn't get enough.

Never enough.

"I love you, Sabrina," he told her in a breathless rush. "You've stolen my heart, and I don't ever want it back."

She rested her hand on his cheek and stared into those fiery blue eyes.

"I love you, Tannis. Even when you're acting crazy. I never knew I could feel this way."

"Crazy for you, babe." The tone of his voice dropped low as he spoke, then he kissed her again.

"So, after all this, we're official?" she asked in a tentative voice, pulling away slightly.

"The jock and the brain? The bad 80s romance movie? Yeah, it's official."

And he gave her that grin, that easy, tempting grin that she fell in love with every time she saw it.

They remained in the backyard in their lingering embrace, trying to recover from the shock of the night and the damage Ken and his cutting words had done.

Damon and Romeo had dragged Ken and his cronies to the front door in heavy discussion, and Ken was gone when they re-entered the house. The whole vibe of the party had shifted and became subdued.

"Bro, I'm gonna have to stop inviting you to my parties," Damon teased as he slapped Tannis's back. "You keep getting into fights."

Damon's dusky gaze brushed over Sabrina who clung to Tannis's side. Damon had been so kind to her, was he about to criticize her now?

Then Damon winked, and cheer and acceptance flooded her body. At least *one* of Tannis's friends accepted her.

"Not that I blame you," Damon continued. He moved in for a bear-hug from Sabrina. "We always got your back, Sabrina," he told her in a low voice. She choked up and bit back tears.

"Yeah, I keep ruining your parties," Tannis admitted with a smile. "How about I promise to be on my best behavior with your next one?"

"Aw shit, Tannis. I've seen you at your ball games. When are you ever on your best behavior?"

Sabrina sat in the bleachers with her backpack resting against her legs, studying her sociology text in between the moments when Tannis was on the field. She clicked her pen out of unconscious habit, the clicking getting lost with each hit when the team's cheering ensued. Her cue to pay attention.

Her phone buzzed and she picked it up to see Diana's name and photo on the screen. Sabrina answered the facetime call.

"I'm on a break from work and wanted to check in on you," Diana's voice squealed over the phone. Her blonde hair was pulled back in a ponytail and she appeared genuinely happy to be talking to Sabrina. *How is she going to make it the rest of summer?* Diana called Sabrina nearly every day.

"No, it's good. We got the car stuff worked out. Tannis put Ken and his friends in their place, so hopefully we won't have to deal with that anymore."

"And look at you, not backing down from it," Diana mused.

The crack of the ball against a bat made Sabrina look up quickly. Not Tannis at bat. *Whew!* She refocused on her phone.

"What does that mean?" Sabrina asked.

"Even at the end of the semester, when Tannis was first crushing on you, you didn't believe something like that could happen. You had this limited view of yourself. I kept telling you that you are cute and strong and more outgoing than you knew, and it just took a few crazy weeks over summer to realize it."

Sabrina nodded at the phone. She hadn't noticed while she was in the thick of it. "I guess you were right."

"Of course, I was. Crap, my break's over. Say hi to Tannis for me."

Then the screen went black, and a text notification from Adele popped up, asking for details from the party. Sabrina exhaled hard at the text. She missed Adele nearly as much as she missed Diana. Sabrina texted her the quick and dirty version, complete with the happy ending. Then Sabrina tucked the phone into her backpack with a smug smile on her face and pretended to study for the rest of Tannis's practice.

When the practice was over, she packed up her books and slung her bag over her arm. Covered in a layer of reddish dust and sweat, Tannis ran to the low chain-link fence and bent way over to reach his lips to hers.

"Hey! I'm glad you made it! Did you like the game? It was just a scrimmage for practice but still . . ."

His eyes were wide and his face so eager and full of hope at her answer, she just couldn't burst his bubble.

"I did love it. Well, most of it, when you were playing."

His lips separated to show his teeth, bright white against his dusty face.

"When you weren't studying," he spoke with a grin, pointing to her bag. Sabrina dipped her head.

"Multi-tasking," she informed him.

Tannis leaned over the fence again, his face close enough that the heat of the game and his excitement wafted onto her cheeks.

"I don't care. You were here, and that's all that matters to me."

Then he pressed forward, brushing his lips against hers in that way that made her heart flutter in her chest.

She tipped her head back and placed a hand on his chest. Her eyes flicked to his upper arm.

"How's the arm? Does it hurt much?"

Tannis did a quick flex and shook his head. "Nope. The team nurse treated it and bandaged it and said I should be fine in a few days with *minimal scarring*, whatever that means."

"Did your coach get pissed at your fighting with a teammate?"

Tannis placed a hand over Sabrina's resting on his chest. "Yeah, a bit. Extra laps and stuff. But he was getting ready to talk to Ken after me, so I got off easy compared to what he'll get. Coach doesn't let stuff like that slide."

"Hey, Reyes!"

A yelling voice carried over the field, and Tannis stiffened and turned, blocking most of Sabrina's view with his body. Of course, this made her curious, and she took a half step to the side to peek around his broad shoulders.

"What do you want, Xiao?" The bite in Tannis's voice could have drawn blood.

Ken's face still bore the reminder of his fight with Tannis, a shadow of purple surrounding his left eye and a bruise on his jaw. Despite her better nature, Sabrina smirked at his injuries, and a swell of pride inflated in her chest.

Don't mess with my man.

Then she blinked and brought herself back around. That wasn't who she was, so she tried to soften the smile, make it welcoming.

Ken held up a hand. "Hey, Tannis. I'm not here to fight. I just want to apologize to you," and he bowed his head at Sabrina, "and you, Sabrina. I was a bit drunk on Saturday, but that's no excuse. I acted badly. I've been acting like an idiot since last semester, and I'm sorry. I just react bad when things change, I guess. If you still hate me, I get it, but I want you to know that I'll be leaving you alone from now on. So will Gabe. And everybody else. Again, I'm sorry."

He then stood there, waiting for something. Tannis's mouth worked, as if he didn't know how to respond until Sabrina bumped him with her shoulder.

"Say something!" she hissed under her breath.

Tannis took a step forward and extended his dust-covered hand.

"Hey, man. I didn't react too hot on Saturday either. I hope I didn't mess you up too bad. And I accept your apology."

Relief flashed across Ken's face, and he gripped Tannis's hand. Then he reached his other hand over to Sabrina.

"I didn't do it, your tires, but people I know did. And since I knew about it, I was complicit. So, I went around to them and made them fork over some Benjamins. Here." He pressed a stack of bills into Sabrina's shocked hand. "I hope it covers what you had to pay for new tires."

Coach Garcia's voice called the players to the center of the field. Sabrina didn't have the chance to say *thank you* before Ken waved at them and ran off. Tannis spun back to Sabrina.

His blue eyes blazed at her, and if possible, she fell in love with him all over again. Just as she seemed to do every day.

"I guess we're in the clear. It looks like we are *bona fide* official. Instead of Romeo and Juliet, we are like Lysander and Hermia."

"Wait, what?"

"You know, from Midsummer Night's Dream?"

Sabrina burst into laughter. "Not quite, but does that make Ken Puck?"

"Well, he sure got everyone in a bunch of trouble, so I guess so."

"Reyes!" Coach Garcia barked.

Tannis pecked Sabrina on her warm cheek.

"I gotta go. Wait for me after?"

"Always," she told him.

Of course, she would wait. He had been so worth the risk.

The End

If you like Campus Romances by M.D Dalrymple, check out the next book in the series – Infatuation – coming soon!

Excerpt from Infatuation

The Hawk's Nest was a dark, cheap, and horribly decorated student bar on the east side of campus. Popular with undergrads, several of his upcoming grad students and another sociology prof had agreed to a meet up before the start of the semester. The dragging, oppressive heat of Southern California's August made any escape from the heat a welcome one, even if it was a college dive bar.

The bar bustled with drinking students and drunk locals, busier than he expected for a Thursday night. Finn Xavier stared at the bar, ordering an old fashioned from the blonde bartender in the tight tank top. The name of the bar was emblazoned across her ample breasts in glittering gemstones, so bright Finn struggled not to stare. She handed his drink over the bar counter, and with a sigh of discontent at leaving the view of her glittery boobs, he wove through the throng of people to a bar-height table in the corner with a view of the door.

Sipping his drink, he scanned the dim interior, looking for any of the students, or Natalie Anza, the other professor. It was after nine. *Shouldn't they be here already?* He glanced at his phone. He had two texts. Group texts.

Crap. Probably cancellations.

And he was right. A student and Natalie. Ugh, if the other two students showed up, he'd be the only faculty in a dumpy student bar. That didn't sound like a fun night to Finn.

Then his phone dinged again, and he didn't have to look at the screen to know what it would read.

But he did. Yep, the other two students canceled.

So here he was, alone at a student bar, sucking on a drink like a creepy guy.

Finn looked down at his shirt. He had even dressed for the night. A deep blue polo to bring out the blue in his green eyes. Fitted jeans to show off his ass and lean legs for, what? What reason? Why did he even dress like this for a meeting with students and one prof who didn't care what he wore?

He swirled the amber liquid in his glass.

Because he was lonely. Teaching, writing, finishing his own PhD, all had kept him too busy to date, to even go out and find someone to hook up with.

When was the last time he'd gotten laid? He sipped the sickly sweet and sour drink.

Months.

No wonder he dressed up. Unconsciously, he was desperate. Was he hoping to hook up with a local? Really? What kind of woman was he going to find at a local dive bar?

I should just leave, Finn thought miserably. Glancing at his drink, he tipped his head, studying it. He did pay for the drink, however, and he had nowhere else to be. Why not apply his own skills and have fun studying this rag-tag group of people?

The college students were easy to identify — young, drinking cheap beer, watching baseball on the big screen and dancing near the jukebox. The local drunks, they sat at the far end of the bar, as far from the college students, focused on their drinks — golden concoctions in highball glasses — not unlike what he was doing. In between sat his point of interest. An eclectic group that could be college students but looking a bit older, drank a myriad of drinks and seemed more interested in laughing and chatting than drinking.

One young woman in particular had a gleam in her dancing brown eyes, a gleam that kept glancing in his direction, at least that's what it seemed to Finn. He ran his fingers through his rich brown hair and leaned his elbows onto the table, suddenly feeling on display. Not that he minded.

His drink was nearly gone, and he'd already decided that he'd hit the road home once he finished.

But he didn't get that chance. The young woman who'd been glancing his way sauntered over, her tight jeans and clinging V-neck shirt leaving little to the imagination. And oh, the things he imagined! What he noticed the most, the sexiest part of her outfit, was the leather collar she wore, one with a slender chain that dipped to her cleavage.

Sexy as hell.

She exuded confidence.

She arrived at his table and sat across from him.

"Have a seat," he told her. She whipped out a side grin that told him she got the joke, and it wasn't a good one.

"Hey, I saw you looking over at us. Are you looking for someone in particular?"

She didn't sound drunk, not even buzzed. Was she a prostitute? That wasn't common to find at a college bar, but stranger things happened in the world.

Most likely she was a student at Mount Laguna College, or the friend or older sister of someone who went there.

Either way, she was dangerous.

From the side smile on her face, she knew how dangerous she was.

And worse, he wanted her. From the minute she'd sashayed over to his table, a flare of desire ripped through him.

And Finn thought she knew that, too.

"Nope. I was going to meet up with some friends, but they all canceled. So, I'm flying solo."

"That's a bummer. I'm Adele." She offered her hand over the table, long fingers with chipped red nail polish.

"Like the singer?" he asked. She nodded. "I'm Finn."

"Finn. Cool name."

"Do you want a drink?" It seemed like the polite thing to ask. She shook her head.

"Nope. My friends have been getting on my nerves. Look, you see?"

She leaned over the table like he had, her highlighted hair brushing against his face. He turned his attention to where she indicated. Finn saw it right away.

Couples. Her friends were coupled up. One couple had their back to him but the other, an athletic looking young man with a black-haired girlfriend, couldn't keep their hands off each other. Finn didn't blame her for searching for other company. She probably felt like a fifth wheel. And as he was alone, he might have looked like a better option than being around people who made her feel more alone than she already did.

Finn understood that too well — loneliness.

"I see it. What, you decided to find some random guy to join instead?"

"Not any random guy. Not like those drunks over there." She cocked her head toward the end of the bar. "I saw you come in, and you only had one drink you were still nursing. So, you didn't come here to get blitzed. You were watching the door, so you were waiting for someone who didn't show. Stood up. That sucks."

Finn's wide eyes stared at this startling woman across from him. She had seen all that? She should be a sociology major, if she was a college student. She was great at reading people. A soc major or a politician.

He smiled at the thought.

"You have a great smile," she told him, her eyes narrowing slightly as they shimmered in the bar light.

Why the hell not? Finn told himself. *I'll bite.*

"Not as great as yours," he replied, hoping it sounded as smooth to her as it had in his head.

Her smile widened. It had sounded as smooth.

"Come on," she said, taking his hand as she stood. Without thinking, he rose.

"Where?"

"Follow me."

Get you copy of Infatuation!

Excerpt from Night Shift

If you like Campus Romances by M.D Dalrymple, you'll also enjoy her police romances – The Men in Uniform Series. Take a peek at *Night Shift:*

THOSE CALLS WERE physically and mentally draining; cops worried during the entire encounter that the drug user would suffer a heart attack in custody and initiate an investigation that, on a cooler day or if the offender abused some other drug, would not happen. Fortunately, last night, no gun was found on either perp, the addicts remained upright, and the booking afterward encountered no glitches.

Matthew recalled the events, evaluating his behavior (wiping his hands on his running shorts in memory of the slimy film that covered the male offender — sometimes the sensation remained even after several showers), checking to make sure he acted by the book. As both offenders were healthy and booked into jail by early morning, Matthew and his brothers in blue considered that a win.

His mind on other matters, he paid little attention as he rounded a sharp curve of the trail. Just as he congratulated himself over a well-executed arrest, a huge German Shepherd ran onto the path, tethered by a long leash. Matthew twisted to the side of the trail to avoid tripping over the dumb beast. The animal emitted one loud bark, and Matthew paused give the dog's owner a dressing down. While he did admire the dog — the animal was a perfect specimen, it could have been a show dog — his mouth, ready to confront the owner, snapped shut.

At the other end of the tethered leash stood a slender, fairly tall woman, bright running shoes extending up to firm, tanned legs. His eyes traveled up her body, over her tiny running shorts that displayed her muscular thighs, over her fitted (*beautifully fitted,* he thought) tank top, to her angular face and sleek, ebony hair pulled back in a tight, low ponytail. Matthew's chest and loins clenched simultaneously, a sensation he had not experienced several years.

The woman reached her hand out to make sure he wasn't going to fall, and Matthew almost took it in his. Shaking his head to clear it, he snatched his hand back.

"You OK?" The woman's liquid voice asked. "Carter just rushed out. He's normally so good and stays by my side, but we haven't gone for a run in several days, and he was excited. I am so sorry."

Concern painted her face. She was rambling, and Matthew bit the inside of his lip to stop a grin.

"No, you are good. I was able to move around him. No blood, no foul."

This time Matthew smiled, and the enchanting woman before him returned the gesture in a radiant glow. Matthew fell into that smile and was lost. He didn't even know her name.

"Beautiful dog," he said, trying to keep her engaged.

Her dark eyes sparkled with pride at the poor dog sitting obediently by her side. Carter kept looking down the trail and back at his mistress, probably wondering, *why aren't we running?*

"Oh, thanks," she replied, reaching to give her good boy a pat, and the dog pressed his head against her leg. The dog obviously loved her unconditionally. Matthew just met her and understood the dog's feelings. The electricity he felt from her burned deep within him.

"May I pet him?" Matthew reached forward and placed his hand at the dog's nose when the woman nodded. "Is he a purebred?"

Her silky hair shimmered as she nodded. "Yep, a gift from my parents when I moved out. They didn't want me living by myself."

"Good choice of a dog for that," Matthew told her. "One of my buddies is in the K9 Unit and cannot stop talking about how amazing the dog is. I've seen his shepherd in action more than once, and Germans are so well trained."

"You've seen a K9 in action? Are you a cop?"

Matthew's smile widened. He loved his job, even after asinine nights like the one before, and enjoyed telling people about it.

"Yeah, out of Tustin."

"Oh, do you live near here, then? Not Tustin? Running and all?" She gestured a slender hand at his running shorts. He had a flashing thought he hoped his package looked tempting.

"Yeah, just west of the park." He held out a hand, praying it wasn't too sweaty. He knew from experience how well *that* went over. "I'm Matthew, by the way."

"Oh, I'm Rosemarie."

Start the Men In Uniform romance series with Night Shift here! Night Shift

And just as a reminder! If you love this book, be sure to leave a review! Reviews are life blood for authors, and I appreciate every review I receive!

Don't forget! If you want more from Michelle? Click the image below to receive three FREE short ebooks, updates, and more in your inbox!

https://linktr.ee/mddalrympleauthor

A Note–

As a college professor, and a former college and grad student, I have a wealth of information about college campus life at my disposal. And since I've been reading more professor-troped romances as of late, I thought to myself, *I have an inside view on this! Why am I not writing these romances for my readers?*

My first book started with something a bit different – a professor and another authority figure on campus: the coach. This book is a more inside look at students – some of the characters are modeled after students I've had in my classes. In this case, the balance of what it is to be an adult and leave the trappings of high school behind, and how some people just can't do that well.

I have about seven or so more books planned for the series, which will include all types of different campus relationship. And each will be a mix of sweet with a good amount of steam! The next book scheduled, *Infatuation*, will have a more traditional college professor/student focus, for those of you looking forward to that.

Thank you for coming along for the ride! I hope you are loving it!

Thank you to my beta and ARC readers for reviews and feedback.

I also have to thank my college friends and colleagues throughout the years who've given me fodder for my writing.

And I want to thank my family and my hubby – my real-world HEA.

About the Author

Michelle Deerwester-Dalrymple is a professor of writing and an author. She started reading when she was 3 years old, writing when she was 4, and published her first poem at age 16. She has written articles and essays on a variety of topics, including several texts on writing for middle and high school students. She is also working on a novel inspired by actual events. She lives in California with her family of seven.

You can visit her blog page, sign up for her newsletter, and follow all her socials at:
https://linktr.ee/mddalrympleauthor

Tempting

Also by the Author:

Glen Highland Romance
The Courtship of the Glen –Prequel Short Novella
To Dance in the Glen – Book 1
The Lady of the Glen – Book 2
The Exile of the Glen – Book 3
The Jewel of the Glen – Book 4
The Seduction of the Glen – Book 5
The Warrior of the Glen – Book 6
An Echo in the Glen – Book 7
The Blackguard of the Glen – Book 8 coming soon!

The Celtic Highland Maidens

The Maiden of the Storm
The Maiden of the Grove
The Maiden of the Celts – coming soon
The Maiden of the Loch – Coming soon
The Maiden of the Stones – Coming soon

Historical Fevered Series – short and steamy romance!

The Highlander's Scarred Heart
The Highlander's Legacy
The Highlander's Return
Her Knight's Second Chance

Tempting

Printed in Great Britain
by Amazon

86471254R00087